Jewish
Latin
America

Jewish Latin America
Ilan Stavans, series editor

THE PROPHET & OTHER STORIES

THE

PROPHET

& Other Stories

SAMUEL RAWET

Translated and with an Introduction by
NELSON H. VIEIRA

University of New Mexico Press
Albuquerque

Library of Congress Cataloging-in-Publication Data
Rawet, Samuel.
    The prophet & other stories / Samuel Rawet : translated and with
an introduction by Nelson H. Vieira.
        p.   cm. — (Jewish Latin America)
    ISBN 0-8263-1837-1 (hardcover). — ISBN 0-8263-1952-1 (pbk.)
    1. Rawet, Samuel—Translations into English. I. Vieira, Nelson.
II. Title. III. Title: Prophet and other stories. IV. Series.
PO9697.R294A28 1998
869.3—DC21   98-23096
                                                                  CIP

The Prophet and Other Stories is the fourth volume in the University of New Mexico
Press series Jewish Latin America.

The statue of the prophet Joel on the title page is by the Brazilian sculptor and
architect Antõnio Francisco Lisboa (1738–1814), known as "O Aleijadinho."

For Nancy,
My Dearest Love

CONTENTS

Translator's Note &
Acknowledgments

In his essay, "The Task of the Translator," Walter Benjamin states that "if translation is a mode, translatability must be an essential feature of certain works." Given that Samuel Rawet's fiction has been virtually unrecognized for many years and, moreover, not translated into English except for two stories, until now, one may wonder about the translatability of his narratives, especially in light of their dense style and elliptical shifts. Despite the translation challenges posed by his work, I of course believe that his fiction is indeed translatable. Hopefully this collection will not only introduce him to a wider English-speaking public, but will also help to restore in part the recognition he so deeply deserves.

To render his voice in a form of English that captures his passionate evocation of the collision of cultures, I have adhered to what Benjamin calls "the interlinear version, in which literalness and freedom are united." Ergo, this translation maintains his long sentences or stories of single paragraphs, frequently sparking the inner and mounting rage of a marginalized or displaced protagonist. In general, I have tried to capture the flavor of his "tugging" style and rich vocabulary. For the most part, I have kept the original names of characters and places. In the case of foreign words such as the Yiddish *sheygetz,* a pejorative term for non-Jew or goy used in "The Prayer," I have changed the spelling of the word in the original Portuguese text to conform to a transliterated Yiddish for English speakers.

The idea for translating Samuel Rawet emerged as a desire to include him in my course, "Prophets in the Tropics: Latin American Jewish Literature-in-Translation." My conversations with his sister, Mrs. Clara Rawet Apelbaum, and her husband, Dr. David Apelbaum, further encouraged me to make his work accessible to a wider public. I wish to acknowledge their assistance in making some of Samuel Rawet's materials available to me as well as their willingness to help me fill in the gaps of his biography. Also, I wish to express my sincere gratitude for their receiving me in their home with graciousness and generosity. As for the project of translation itself, I am profoundly indebted to two individuals. First, to my wife, Nancy Levitt-Vieira, for carefully examining the manuscript and for offering innumerable suggestions to improve its readability. Her contribution to this project has been invaluable. And, secondly, to Marcus Vinicius de Freitas, assistant professor at the Federal University of Minas Gerais, who not only served as my native informant, but who gave generously of his time in helping me to decipher some of the difficult passages. I am appreciative of his camaraderie and friendship. For giving me a Brazilian base to develop and discuss my research on Samuel Rawet, I am grateful to my colleagues in two research units at the Federal University of Rio de Janeiro—the Interdisciplinary Center for Contemporary Study (CIEC), especially to Dr. Ilana Strozenberg (director), and to my dear friend and colleague, Professor Heloísa Buarque de Hollanda, director of the Advanced Program of Contemporary Culture (PACC). Thanks also to my colleagues for their continual support and, especially, to Professor Onésimo T. Almeida, Chair of the Department of Portuguese and Brazilian Studies, Brown University. Finally, I would like to thank Ilan Stavans, the editor of this series on Latin American Jewish writers, for his support of this project and his enthusiasm for Rawet's fiction.

—N.H.V.

INTRODUCTION

"That total asininity of not seeing the other face of everyday reality."
SAMUEL RAWET, "THE LAND OF ONE SQUARE INCH"

As the proclaimed pioneer of Brazilian-Jewish writing, Samuel Rawet (1929–84) represents an artfully sensitive voice of the Jewish Diaspora in Latin America, specifically Brazil, a country of more than 150 million inhabitants that today harbors between 120,000 and 150,000 Jews whose ancestry is primarily Eastern European. Although Jews have been coming to Portuguese-speaking South America since the early part of the sixteenth century, soon after the discovery of Brazil in 1500, those colonial Jews arrived as "simulated" New Christians, a rubric indicative of the forced colonization of their religion and culture that took place in Catholic Iberia prior to their departure for the New World. Consequently, once in Brazil, one may interpret their status as precolonized colonizers, reflective not only of their enforced simulation as New Christians, but also of the ensuing "dissimulation" adopted by many Crypto-Jews who chose to express clandestinely their Judaic heritage and religion.

This historical backdrop partially explains the eventual disappearance of their Sephardic culture via centuries of obligatory assimilation. In view of these historical circumstances, the modern-day presence of Jews in Brazil is the result of late-nineteenth and twentieth-century immigration which had no direct link to the colonial Jewish population. This history also explains why the ancestry of the contemporary Brazilian-Jewish population stems, in the majority, not from Sephardic origins, but from the persecuted Ashkenazi Jews of Eastern Europe. In Rawet's life and in his stories, this historical persecution leads to the heartwrenching experience of dispersion, exile, immigration, and alienation. And it is the heightened consciousness of being "other"—dramatized in the immigrant, the marginal figure, the Wandering Jew, the oppressed son, or the subaltern—that is the hallmark of Rawet's fiction and his discourse of difference. Sensitive to the hazards of all forms of absolutist thinking, Samuel Rawet allegorizes in his writing an ethics of quest, openness, freedom, change, and difference that challenges the tyranny of ethnocentrism, homogeneity, and rigid subjectivity.

If Samuel Rawet's fiction represented in 1956 the recognized genesis[1] of the uninhibited literary expression of the Jewish experience in Brazil, despite the prior publication of primarily documentary-type narratives of Jewish immigration by a few lesser-known writers, then perhaps his provocative and penetrating stories may in part redeem the lost voices of the Jewish culture of enforced silence, unjustified neglect, and historical invisibility that became "absented" in colonial Brazil. Furthermore, his writing questions the behavior shown toward "ethnic others" who do not reflect Brazil's predominantly Christian culture and its traditional mores. In other words, on the deep structural level, Rawet's fiction evokes the difficulties of reconciling Jewish beliefs and culture with Brazilian nationalist norms. In addition, his initial depiction of Jewish and Yiddishkeit culture in Brazil and, by extension, the universal experience of all immigrants and subalterns, points to his being one of the first notable and publicly acknowledged Brazilian-Jewish voices speaking in modern literature via the Portuguese language. Along these lines, his Brazilian literature of Jewish expression offers the contemporary reader an opportunity to appreciate the articulation of a Jewish identity within the Latin American context, particularly within the frame of Brazil's multicultural and multiracial society, where "to be or not to be Jewish" becomes not only a question of situational ethnicity and cultural negotiation, but also a perennial dilemma for Brazilian Jews facing assimilationist ideologies of nationalism and insidious expressions of prejudice that do not easily accommodate cultural differences.

Samuel Rawet was born in Klimontow, a small Polish town near Warsaw that was eventually destroyed during World War II.[2] He emigrated to Brazil at the age of seven and with his family settled in the northern proletariat suburbs of Rio de Janeiro, away from the lushness of the city's tropical beauty of green mountains and sparkling beaches. Rawet's father had arrived in Brazil earlier in 1933, seeking a better life for his wife and children. He left his family behind, including four-year old Samuel, in a *shtetl*, or little village of Polish Jews whose livelihood consisted of small trade in the town's bustling marketplace. Rawet had many memories of his early education in a Jewish *heder* (school) in this premodern Yiddishkeit existence. Allusions have been made to the enduring family tensions in the Rawet household that resulted from the father's emigration and his temporary separation from his wife and children, personal tensions that troubled family harmony later in Brazil. Interestingly, the conflict between fathers and sons is repeatedly dramatized in many of Rawet's stories with symbolic intimations of the potentially violent biblical story of the *akedah*, the binding of Isaac by his father Abraham.

Rawet referred to his memory of his past *shtetl* existence as one reminiscent of the daily life of the original Hasidic movement. Also, he incorporated into his own philosophy and set of ethics the philosophical writings of Martin Buber. An avid reader and cultured man of letters, Rawet recalled his premodern Yiddishkeit childhood as well as the Judaic lifestyle of his adolescence in Brazil, with the emphasis upon learning and scholasticism, as cultural values important to his development as a writer. Practicing Judaism regularly until he was fifteen, Rawet lived in various suburbs and neighborhoods teeming with Jews and other immigrants. It is this cross-cultural ambiance and life experience that served as the inspiration for his first collection of stories *Contos do imigrante* (1956) [Tales of the Immigrant]. This collection launched Rawet's career and gave him national recognition because it was published by Rio's prestigious José Olympio Editora. However, this success was short-lived since his four subsequent collections and two novellas were published by increasingly smaller presses that displayed little or no means for effective marketing and distribution. Furthermore, the nonmainstream themes of his fiction and the sociocultural and political climate of Brazil's military rule of the late 1960s and early 1970s made it more difficult for Rawet to find publishers for his literature. Moreover, with the authoritarian regime's circumscribed notion of culture that did little to support the arts, much less the art of Brazilian "subcultures," his publications found no viable public and so his work began to slip into literary oblivion.

During his late teens and early twenties, Rawet became a voracious reader who began to discover international as well as national writers. Appreciating such Brazilian authors as the regionalist Graciliano Ramos and the early-twentieth-century mulatto writer Lima Barreto (also a resident of Rio's depressing suburbs), Rawet developed a sense of their craft as well as that of foreign writers such as Mann, Hesse, Kafka, Wasserman, Dostoyevsky, and Gorky.

Later, he enrolled in the National School of Engineering and received his degree in 1953. During his university years he began to write short stories and plays and witnessed at close hand the burgeoning years of modern Brazilian theater. He became involved in the *Movimento dos Novos*, the Movement of Young Writers, who were linked to a small literary circle called *Café da Manhã*. This group became his literary family, ultimately inspiring his career as a writer. However, it became evident to the others of this circle that, despite his collaboration in various literary projects, Rawet was very much a loner who desperately needed daily solitude. His solitary stance affected him increasingly throughout his personal and professional life and became an emblem of his overall way of being.

Knowing that he could not support himself with his writing, Rawet made the decision to follow a more lucrative profession. In 1957 he was invited to Brasília, the nation's new capital in the interior, as an engineer to join NOVACAP, the famous architectural team of Oscar Niemeyer and company. Rawet participated in this epic enterprise by specializing in the mathematical calculation of reinforced concrete, the material used for Brasília's futuristic buildings. At the same time, he cultivated an appreciation for Brasília's vast plateau and the spacious solitude of this new frontier which resulted in his reputation as an incessant loner, a Jew wandering and writing in the silence and solitude that came with the new capital's cultural isolation.

In the early sixties he decided to travel to other parts of the country. He explored the new Belém-Brasília highway and interior cities such as Manaus in the Amazon. In 1964, he sold some of his possessions and bought passage on a transatlantic ship to Europe. He visited Portugal, France, Italy, and Israel, a trip which inspired several of the stories in this collection. When he returned to Brasília, he spent the next decade in gradual isolation, alienating himself more and more from friends, family, and the Jewish community of Brazil. In 1981 after a decade of relative silence, he published one last collection, *Que os mortos enterrem os mortos* [Let the Dead Bury the Dead], a series of stories depicting many lonely, disturbed, and paranoid characters. Reclusive and compulsive, he distanced himself from everyone with each passing year. Finally, living alone in a spartanly furnished, rented apartment in Sobradinho, one of the small satellite cities of Brasília's southern wing, he died of a cerebral aneurysm.

At the time of Rawet's death in 1984, the Brazilian-Jewish journalist and writer Alberto Dines wrote an article proclaiming Rawet "the inventor of exile," in response to critical statements about his supposed anti-Jewish stance. In this publication, Dines deftly captured Rawet's insider/outsider plight and his feelings of exile and solitude: "He gave us immigrant literature, he lived in exile—where else could he die but on the banks of the rivers of Babylon, forgotten, self-absorbed, lost."[3] Contesting the accusations about Rawet's perceived anti-Semitism and at the same time revealing some of the key characteristics of Rawet's personality, Dines emphatically stated: "Rawet, an anti-Semite? Have the Jews changed so much that their inventor in modern Brazilian literature is seen as anti-Jewish? He who opted for deprivation, for humility, for simplicity of life, he who was all thought, dispossessed—exactly like the Prophets—solely dedicated to an understanding of the world, could that tenderness for the solitary and marginal beast be anti-Semitic? I doubt it."

Although recognizing Rawet's mounting paranoia and hypertension, Dines also heralded his literary vision—agnostic and antagonistic yet vanguardist, very much in tune with his hermetic and dense style. It is not an exaggeration to state that Rawet's life and fiction manifested the difficulties, misconceptions, and tragedies of cross-cultural conflict and despair, indicative of lives in dispersion. His literature recalls an incisive statement made by the self-exiled Jewish-American painter R. B. Kitaj, who wrote the *First Diasporist Manifesto* (1989): "A Diasporist picture is marked by Exile and its discontents as subtly and unclearly as pictures by women or homosexuals are marked by their inner exilic discontents."

However, while cross-cultural conflicts dominate most of the stories in his first collection, he extended his theme of immigration and cultural conflict into the broader universal subject of displacement, strangeness, and otherness. Rawet's alienated, searching, and decentered gaze at the world, frequently described in a hermetic, dense, perplexing, and elliptical style, designed to reflect the pulsating intensity of troubled souls, represents his lasting and unique contribution to Brazilian literature.

Instead of reading his fiction as "narrative disorder," as an unenlightened critic once declared, one may appreciate his innovative syntax and special use of time, space, and language as techniques for conveying the sense of dislocation, confusion, anger, and isolation endemic to the complex and elusive web of being "other." In this context, his style reminds one of Deleuze and Guattari's term, the "deterritorialization" of language, an aspect of "minor literature or expression" of a different cultural ethos embedded in a dominant one, a type of cultural dislocation seen as "disjunction between content and expression."[4] Rawet's new way of using language resisted rigid interpretation by inviting the reader to participate actively. Rawet's act of writing entails knowing or implying what it feels like to write in a language that originally is not one's own, just as a reader may learn to know what it feels like to live in a culture that is not entirely his or her own.

The selection of stories for this collection was designed to provide the English-speaking public with a representative corpus of some of Rawet's best narratives as well as an indication of his development as a writer. They also constitute the first volume of his stories in English translation. Only two other of his narratives have been translated into English—the story "His Moment of Glory" and a portion of his last novella, "Ahasverus." The twelve stories selected here for translation are drawn from four separate collections. The first four stories— "The Prophet," "The Prayer," "Judith," and "Little Gringo"—were chosen because they are part of Rawet's inaugural and most famous collection, *Contos do imigrante* (1956). Also, these four stories feature many aspects of Jewish immigration in Brazil and, to date, constitute some of the best narratives on this experience. The next three stories—"Dialogue," "Christmas Without Christ," and "Parable on the Son and the Fable"—are from the collection, *Diálogo* (1963) [Dialogue]. Here, the reader will observe that some stories deal directly with the Jewish question in Brazil while others do not overtly refer to their protagonists as Jews. In some cases, they may be Jews but the ambiguity is deliberately constructed so that the reader may think beyond ethnic boundaries. While the story "Dialogue" hints at the Jewish ethnicity of the father and son, "Christmas Without Christ" does treat directly the insider/outsider dilemma of being Jewish in Brazil, while "Parable on the Son and the Fable" takes a more universal position on the generation gap. Interestingly, the act of telling fables as a means of unilaterally shaping children's lives is ironically treated in both "Dialogue" and "Parable." The next three stories— "The Seven Dreams," "Faith in One's Craft," and "The First Cup of Coffee"—stem from the collection *Os sete sonhos* (1967) [The Seven Dreams], a volume of disparate tales that reveal a more cerebral, less emotional bent. These stories differ considerably from the poignancy found in his first collection and reveal the trajectory and development of Rawet's art. Here an evocatively oneiric narration, "The Seven Dreams," appears with the ironic and playful metafictional tale, "Faith in One's Craft," as well as a touching but slightly humorous immigrant story, "The First Cup of Coffee." The last two stories—"Johny Golem," and "Lisbon By Night"—are from the collection *O terreno de uma polegada quadrada* (1969) [The Land of One Square Inch], which contains one novella bearing the title of the volume, plus ten stories. This collection also represents a departure from Rawet's dense and ambiguous style because, while these two stories also deal with Jewish themes, they present a more direct depiction of scene and character that includes touches of humor, social satire, and Rawet's ongoing philosophical pursuit of ontological questions.

In the first four stories about the tribulations of Jewish immigration in Brazil, the issue of cross-cultural conflict is underscored. However, it is interesting to note that, in the case of "Judith," the conflict focuses upon an intracultural problem, suggesting the potential dangers of rigid ethnocentrism. The title story for this collection, "The Prophet," is a favorite story that has appeared in several Brazilian anthologies. This retrospective tale, presented primarily from the old man's point of view, is framed by scenes of his departure on board ship. When the narrative unexpectedly shifts back to his arrival in Brazil, the reader accompanies the old man as he expresses his contradictory feelings about his materialistic family in Brazil. As a mocked "prophet" and holocaust survivor, he is not only seen as a curiosity, but he also provides no fulfilling prophecy. This reality is reinforced by his inability to speak Portuguese. For all purposes, he is a "prophet" with no language.

In *Dialogue*, Rawet has created an ironic series of stories in which no meaningful dialogue actually occurs between people, in these cases, between father and son, ethnic and native, parents and children. In the title story, the tension between father and son is related via the son's thoughts which reveal the father's potential violence just like Isaac and Abraham in the biblical story of the *akedah*. However, this story conveys a displaced *akedah*, for there is no redemption or reconciliation between these two. Rawet's approach to this story suggests his use of inversion to deconstruct patriarchal and cultural myths that profess democracy and harmony. The dialogical discourse implied in the title actually takes place between reader and text rather than between the fictional characters. In "Christmas Without Christ," Rawet juxtaposes Christian logocentrism with class and socially rooted authoritarianism to deconstruct the hypocrisy and insensitivity of a bourgeois Catholic family. Inversion and irony are also used here to show the distinction between obvious prejudice and masked discrimination, practices that often confuse or muddle the actual state of racial and ethnic relations in Brazil.

The collection *The Seven Dreams,* presents in the title story an unusual dream sequence that plays with the mystical number of seven as well as with the oneiric and mutable roles an individual may experience. The effect of evoking a series of elusive dreams may provoke in the reader thoughts about the elusiveness of reality as well as questions about the sovereignty of a fixed subjectivity.

And with the self-conscious metafictional narrative, "Faith in One's Craft," a writer discusses the process of writing which offers no concession to literary conventions. Here, ambiguity and contradiction are the paradoxical experiences in life that allow for no certifications and assurances. And so it is more important to have faith in one's craft or art than to seek some circumscribed idea or convention of what art should be.

With the last two stories, Rawet again reverts to themes integral to Jewish culture—the *golem,* the figure of clay in Jewish mysticism created to protect Jews from the fury of their enemies, and the Jewish Question about allegiance to one's ethnic origins and/or to one's country. In "Johny *Golem,*" the Frankenstein theme of the creature rebelling against the creator is inverted to illustrate the practice of exploitation, in this case, against a mock Jewish *golem,* actually a disturbed Jewish schizophrenic who, instead of being a figure of protection, becomes a victim of abuse. A satire on the scientific method and manipulative research, this story is told with humor as well as irony. In the final piece, "Lisbon by Night," the story of dual allegiance and ethnic prejudice or discrimination is narrated straightforwardly but with an ending that leaves the reader with questions about the protagonist's position. With the name of Isaac being used, the protagonist becomes another modern-day inversion of the biblical *akedah* because his encounter with pernicious evil suggests that there is little hope for salvation or redemption.

In conclusion, the translated stories of this collection all relate to the vicissitudes of displaced individuals who, owing to immigration, prejudice, and marginalization, are frequently trapped by mindsets that cultivate stereotypes and maintain the status quo. These stories challenge a society's rigid norms and the types of cultural ideologies that operate in absolutes. In other words, Rawet's stories stimulate ideas about social consciousness as a means of avoiding the temptation to see life in absolutist terms. Just as the protagonist in his last novella, *Viagens de Ahasverus . . .* (1970) [Travels of Ahasverus] experiences perpetual change through a series of willed metamorphoses that evoke a metamorphic otherness, many of the characters in these stories, to varying degrees, via their sense of exile, alienation, and displacement, embody a consciousness that begs for more acceptance and inclusion of cultural differences. As a prophetic, solitary Brazilian-Jewish voice writing about multicultural issues, *avant la lettre*, during the first decades of the second half of the twentieth century, Samuel Rawet knew all too well that we can all be others and strangers, even in our own land.

N.H.V.

Providence, RI, 1997

NOTES

1. When speaking about Jewish literary expression in Brazil, Jacob Guinsberg, the Brazlian publisher and critic, declared in 1957 that Rawet's *Tales of the Immigrant* "characterizes the de jure appearance of this subject in our literature." Reprinted in *Shalom* (September 1984): 8–10.

2. For a more detailed account of Samuel Rawet's life and writings, see Nelson H. Vieira, *Jewish Voices in Brazilian Literature: A Prophetic Discourse of Alterity* (Gainesville: University Press of Florida, 1995), pp. 51–99.

3. See Alberto Dines, "Inventor do exílio" [The inventor of exile], *Shalom* (1984): 4–5.

4. See Gilles Deleuze and Félix Guattari, *Kafka: Toward a Minor Literature*, translated by Dana Polan (Minneapolis: University of Minnesota Press, 1986), p. 20.

THE PROPHET

All illusions lost, the only thing really left for him to do was to take that step. The gangplank already hauled off, and the last whistle blown, the steamship would weigh anchor. He again looked at the cranes wielding bales, the piles of ore and other minerals. Down below, people hustling and bustling and foreign tongues. Necks stretched out in cries toward those who surrounded him on the rampart of the upper deck. Handkerchiefs. In the distance, the honking of automobiles revealing the life that continued on in the city he was now abandoning. The sneering looks of some mattered little to him. At another time he would have felt hurt. He understood that the white beard and the long overcoat well below his knees made him a strange figure to them. He had become accustomed to that reaction. Right now they would be laughing at the thin figure, all in black except for the face, the beard, and the even whiter hands. However, no one dared challenge those eyes that commanded respect and instilled a certain majestic air to his demeanor. With fists folded against his temples, he resisted interior escape into the serenity that had brought him to this point. Hearing the ship's muffled toot, he became fully aware of his plunging into solitude. The return, the only way out he had discovered, seemed to him empty and illogical. He thought, at the moment of hesitation, that he had acted as a child. Lately, the idea had been building into gigantic proportions and had culminated in his presence on board the ship. Now he was afraid of seeing that decision effaced by the glimmer of doubt. The fear of solitude terrified him more so because of the experience obtained in his daily contact with death. There was still time . . .

"Step down the gangplank, please, step down!"

The fat figure of the woman to his side turned upon hearing, or upon thinking that she heard, the words of the old man.

"Sir, did you say something to me?"

Useless. He knew the language barrier would not allow him to say anything. The woman's face changed with the old man's negative nod and supplicating eyes. With exceptions, the true recourse would be mimicry but that would accentuate the childishness that tyrannized him. Only then did he realize he had murmured the sentence, and ashamed, he closed his eyes.

"My wife, my children, my son-in-law."

Confused, he gazed at the group that kept on hugging and kissing, a strange group (even his brother and cousins, if not for the photographs mailed ahead, would also seem strange to him), and the tears then rolling down his cheeks were not of tenderness but of gratitude. He had known the older ones as children. Thirty years ago his own brother was little more than an adolescent. Here he had married, had sons and daughters, and had also seen his daughter marry. Not even after settling into the cushioned springs of the car the son-in-law was driving did his tears stop flowing. To the onslaught of questions, he responded with gestures, evasions, or else silence. Despite its age, his thin but hard body had enabled him to work and, moreover, had saved his life. Now it swayed with the traffic's hesitations and never once did his eyes gaze upon the landscape. He seemed to be concentrating more on responding to the avalanche of tenderness. What was going on inside would be impossible for him to convey through the superficial contact now being initiated. He figured his silences were embarrassing. The silences following the series of questions about himself, about the most terrifying thing he had experienced. To forget what had happened, never. But how to belittle it, to eliminate the essence of the horror as one sat down to a beautifully set table, or as one sipped tea ensconced in elegant cushions and comfortable armchairs? The avid and inquiring eyes around him, hadn't they heard or seen enough to be horrified as well and to share his silences? One world alone. He expected to find on this side of the ocean the comfort of those like him who had suffered, but whom chance had marginally saved from the worst. And being conscious of that, they shared this meeting with humility. However, he had an inkling of a slight mistake on his part.

The apartment occupied by his brother was on the top floor of the building. Open to the sea, the veranda absorbed the nightly crash of the waves with more furor than during the day. There he liked to sit (having returned from the synagogue after evening prayers) with his grandnephew on his lap, both babbling nonsense. The child's fingers would get tangled in his beard and sometimes forcibly grope for a tuft of hair or two. Pincus would then rub his hard nose with his roundish and cartilaginous finger and both of them would let loose a carefree laugh. They would amuse themselves until the time the brother got home and they went in to dinner.

During the first weeks there was much commotion and many houses to visit, many tables to eat at, and in all the homes he felt indignant for being taken for granted as a *curiosity*. With time, once the enthusiasm and the curiosity had cooled down, he ended up spending time only with his brother. Actually talking only to him or to his wife. The others hardly understood him, nor did his nephews, and even less so the son-in-law, toward whom he began to nurture a real aversion.

"Here comes the 'Prophet'!"

He had barely opened the door when the son-in-law's derisive words and laugh surprised him. He pretended as if he hadn't noticed the others' uneasiness. He had taken his time on the way home from the synagogue and they were already waiting for him at the dinner table. He glimpsed his brother's disapproval and one of the children's shortened laugh. Only Paulo (that's how they called the grandson, whose real name was Pincus) moved his hands babbling as though to complain about the lost playtime. Mute, he placed his hat on the rack, keeping only the black silk cap on his head. He still hadn't learned a thing about the language. But, being a good observer, even though he didn't dare say anything, by association he managed to memorize a few things. And the word "prophet," delivered with mischievous laughter as he came into the house, was becoming familiar. He didn't get its meaning. Little did it matter, however. The word was never uttered without an ironic look, a smirk. In the bathroom (while he was washing his hands) he was reminded of the innumerable times the same sounds were said in front of him. He made the connection with other scenes. From down deep surfaced the memory of something similar having occurred in the temple.

The mistake he sensed on the first day became more pronounced. The sensation that their world was really something other than his— that they had not participated in anything that (for him) had been the horrible night—was being slowly transformed into concrete reality. The dinner gatherings where he would remain in the background were to him quite tiresome. When the children were sleeping and the other couples came over to chat, he felt foolish listening to the tone of the conversation, the bawdy jokes, the numbers always being bandied about in reference to everything and, at times, to nothing. The war had stripped him of all his prior illusions and had confirmed the precariousness of what once had been solid. The only thing remaining intact had been his faith in God and in religion, so deep-rooted that even during the most bitter ordeals he hadn't been able to expel his belief. (He had already tried, he knew, but in vain.) A year had scarcely gone by and he found himself still repeating monotonously what he imagined to be over and done with. The son-in-law's parasitic situation awakened in him feelings of hatred, and at great expense, he controlled himself. He had seen other hands making other gestures. But the manicured nails and the rings, the roly-poly body, the stupid laugh, and his uselessness intensified his overall disgust. How many times (long past midnight), on the veranda with his cigarette lit, he would let himself forget while listening to the vulgar (to him) guffaws uttered bilingually from one card game to another.

"So this is what it's all about?"

The others thought it was senility. He knew very well it wasn't. Monologues had been useful to him when he thought he was going crazy. Today they were a habit. When alone, he would release tension by saying one sentence or another with no meaningful connection, except for him. He remembered one day (right in the beginning), in the middle of some conversation, he had half-heartedly attempted some flimsy complaint by making some weak sign of protest, and perhaps his index finger did cut the air with gestures of ominous intentions. The same thing in the synagogue when the congregation's rudeness had disturbed a prayer.

"Those fat, bossy men of plenty don't belong here," he had murmured to himself one day.

Perhaps for that reason, the *prophet*. (Afterwards he had discovered its meaning.)

He thought about changing a little his topics of conversation and began to narrate stories about what he had once denied. But now it didn't seem to interest them. Condescendingly (they didn't understand what degree of sacrifice that meant to him) they listened to him at first and no tears were missing from the women's eyes. Afterwards, noticing their annoyance, indignation, he thought he discovered reproof in some looks and second guessed sentences like these: "What do you expect from all this talk? Why do you torment us with stuff that has nothing to do with us?" There were wrinkles of remorse when they remembered someone who was connected to them, yes. But these moments were brief. They disappeared as a crease does in a rubber doll. It didn't take long for such behavior to become obvious, albeit masked.

"You are suffering from all this talk. Why do you insist so?"

He shut up. And more than that, he became silent. Very seldom did they hear a word from him, and they didn't notice that he was putting himself into a marginal situation. Only Pincus (that's what he called him) continued to braid his beard, rub his nose, and tell endless stories with his round eyes. Uselessness.

The sea brought back sad memories and launched enigmatic ones. Solitude upon solitude. At times, he asked himself about his capacity to last in an environment that was no longer his. The whoosh of the waves. A small finger plunged into his mouth and then a laugh at the jolt. An unrestrained laugh. Did he have the right to condemn? Not really, if this was pleasurable reward after the torment. No, he couldn't even condemn himself if for some reason he gave in, despite his age. But the others? Blind and deaf in their insensitivity and self-sufficiency! He'd then get up. He'd walk through the rooms, examining the household comfort for signs of contrast he knew beforehand did not exist. He lured himself into useless arguments. And from down deep came a bitter and disappointing taste. The days piled up in a routine manner but the time in the synagogue on Saturdays was painful for him. With his prayer book open (unnecessary since he uttered all the prayers by heart), he would close his eyes to the intrigues and would remain to the side, always to the side. On his way home, he would admire the showy colors of the shop windows, the skyscrapers disappearing in the distance with the turn of his neck, and the incessant crawl of the automobiles. And in the midst of all that, solitude weighed him down, the spiritual state that had not found any affinity whatsoever.

He knew his brother's good fortune to be recent. In one of his rare moments of rest, he had told him about the years of struggle in the suburbs, and triumphant, with sweeping gestures, he capped his story with the success of his present security. More than any other sensations, that one affected him profoundly, echoing deep inside. He realized that any kind of affinity was impossible since their experiences were totally opposite. His, bitter. The other's, victorious. And in the same interim of time!? God, my God! Nights of insomnia followed. He tried to reach the conclusion that a feeling of envy had burdened him with hatred. Impossible. Being really honest with himself, he easily saw right through that conclusion. And stood by the opposite one, the more difficult one. The forms in the dimness of the room (he slept with the grandson) composed scenes he didn't expect to see again. Horrible and skeletal daybreaks. Anguished faces and prayers flying away from human ashes. His wife's figure wrapping her shawl at the last minute. Where are the eyes, where are the muted eyes that disclosed the animal cry? Roguish laughter. Card games. Numbers. Look at the "prophet" over there! And faces of laughter, giggling at the overcoat draped on the chair. Impossible.

The increasing cries made him notice the time of departure. He looked at the docks. Slowly the strip of water expanded with the final gestures of good-bye. He tightened all the muscles in his body. When the family returned from the resort, they would find his letter on the table. And the protests would be useless because they were too late. He had taken advantage of their two-week absence. The passport with his tourist visa (after, they were thinking about changing it for a permanent one) made his plan easy. The money he owned was all spent on the ticket. Return. The maid found it a bit strange to see him leave with his suitcase. But she attributed the fact to the eccentric figure who in the beginning had instilled in her a little fear. Plans? He didn't have any. He was simply going in search of the company of people who were the same, the same, yes. Perhaps in search of the end. The energies this step demanded had wiped him out, and his debilitated state had brought some doubts. And facing the irremediable, his frustrated eyes swelled in the anxious attempt to quell his tears. Already tiny by now, the figures waving good-bye. The mountainous background, bluish in the midday sky. Green blocks of little islands and spray on the bows of the barges. (There are always seagulls. But he couldn't see them.) Again, his fists closing and moving crosswise, his head resting in his arms, and the black figure, in the form of a hook, trembling in tears.

THE PRAYER

At the entrance to the courtyard, the remains of a wall nobody ever bothered to raise after it was knocked down by a truck, Zico assembled the gang of boys.

"There, the old woman, over there!"

Turning the corner, the black shawl wrapped around her neck while her rough hands stiffened on either side of her body, weighed down by two immense packages. The quick pace, firm footsteps of heelless shoes, cut across the line of vision of the startled boys who only saw her marked profile and her grey hair pulled back into a bun. They never had the courage to look her straight in the eyes, and when they threw the first stone, scraping her feet, they expected to hear her half-baked babble but encountered only a pale expression and a twisted mouth. The anticipated and frustrated pleasure left them always wanting more. That's why they looked at her sideways, or sometimes spied on her through the window. There wasn't anyone like her in the building. Zico, the oldest, guaranteed it. He knew the thirty or so residents of the tenement and never had he heard speak of a similar case. The old woman arrived suddenly, just a few days ago, silently. She arranged her belongings, which a black man had carried on his head, in the one room apartment in back, and without having spoken to anyone, she came and went, mute, her shoes damaging the corridor's rotting woodwork. Only once did they hear her voice. On the second day after her arrival she went to ask for matches from old Genoveva, who was lighting her pipe, seated on a bench and taking a break from her washing. Genoveva opened a half closed eye, freed her mouth and smiled with a half dozen teeth scattered over her gums. She found it hard to understand what the foreigner wanted. "Please . . . Lend . . . ," her fingers scratched the palm of her hand, and in her pleading eyes a fear of the laughter the neighborhood kids were mustering. "I make . . . ," strange mimicry expressed haltingly, the missing word. Genoveva stretched her arm which the old woman grabbed tightly and taking the matchbox she raced off. The noise of their voices rattled her. Brito, the boldest, aped her gestures and jumbled his words, while the others, in back, laughed foolishly. "You . . . good-for-nothing . . . *sheygetz* . . . " The bun turned around and elicited a hailstorm of jolting responses. Worse. The laughter increased. The joking as well. Brito, scratching his belly, guffawed, continuing the dialogue with shrills and howls, interspersed with some barking. While she climbed the steps, a rock scraped against her ankle. The turn of the bun poured forth a pale expression and the twisted mouth. Sudden silence. Brito scratched his belly in slow motion until he stopped.

Instantaneously a heaviness immobilized them until her sturdy steps were again heard on the floorboards of the corridor, and Genoveva's frightening scream:

"Out on the street right now, you low life!!!"

She fell down on the bed alongside the packages. A relief rose from her fingertips, ran up her shoulder blades, and escaped through her mouth in a sigh. She rubbed her face and burning cheeks. She was neither used to this kind of sun, nor to this type of drudgery. The perspiration made her feel uncomfortable inside and from her armpits a soggy triangle ran to its vertex at her waist. Taste of sand in her mouth. Her elbows on her knees, her face in the palm of her hands, she panted, parched, grim, sad. The black shawl on her thighs flooded her vision. Friday! Four o'clock! My God! She turned her face. Through the closed window came a wave of heat, floating on to the bed, the table, the junky bureau, beating and beating again against the walls, concentrating solidly upon Ida's body. A desire to stay there chained to the bed, to fuse fatigue and solitude. Friday. Four o'clock. My God! She broke through her inertia by tearing off her shoes. She slid her aching feet into her slippers and breaking through her lethargy went to the sink. Friday.

She lifted the cover of the pan and a steaming smell of cooked meat warmed her face. She stoked the coal stove, revived the fire with more coal and a fan, and in a pan of boiling water she dumped the two slices of fish. From the chest of drawers came a white cloth for the table. A different aroma flooded the room, now cleaned and swept. On the bed she ripped open the packages, arranging in boxes, the stockings, handkerchiefs, pieces of soap, packages of hairpins, shoe-laces, ribbons . . . a whole world! Her world. On the wall Isaiah's praying eyes had been startled by the click of the photograph. Ida remembered the trouble in convincing him to keep the photo that was taken by surprise. Now, all yellowed, it hung on the wall, showing the blot of his beard, his arched eyebrows and those startled eyes. From the others nothing more had remained. Ida's eyes quivered with the memory. What a nightmare! On Fridays Isaiah would come home more happy, his face shining, and one drop of water or another from his beard would be a sign of the ritual bath. He would gently slap her on the back a few times, (Ida's face was red from the wood in the stove), and would go pray. Now only the photograph.

An uproar in the courtyard. Scampering throughout the building. Shouts, singing coming from the communal washbasin. A radio on the upstairs floor poured out sambas. Amidst the commotion, standing still by the window Ida was lost, without language, without voice. Forced into a life that never had been hers. Her whole body still aching from the walking. Climbing and descending streets, steps, neighborhoods. Walking. And being alone. Ida felt a tiredness flood her soul. Children, she had already had them, husband as well. From all that, only the photo on the wall remained. And herself. On her wrinkled face, a crushed suffering. She was forgetting. All of them died in the war. Rattled by the steam, the pan's cover beat to the samba on the radio. Without knowing how she disembarked in this port. She was leaving a whole existence behind. Ave-Maria coming from the upstairs floor and the room practically in darkness. At the beginning they invited her to stay at somebody's house, but as a novelty, a rare beast from other lands who has stories lasting for more than a month. The stories wore out. So did the kindness. Then came the tenement with a language she did not understand, kids making fun of her, the packages burdening her arms, and her legs registering sidewalks and rubbing together daily over a hundred doormats. The light from a streetlamp split Ida's face in two, diagonally. One eye blinded by the flash of light glowed moistlessly. Feeling her way, she dragged her feet to the light switch. From one drawer, unwrapping the flannel, she took out two silverplated candlesticks and caressed them tremulously. On the table, she arranged the candles without noticing some small eyes squeezed together, breath held, glued to the window. She tied an enormous white kerchief on her head and, with the candles lit, she closed her eyes and swayed her body back and forth.

"Didja see?"

"I saw! . . . The gringa acted in a strange way! . . . "

"You were a dope! . . . You should have thrown a rock at the window."

"Don't be a jerk! One thing is really bothering me . . . "

"What ?"

"This business with the candle . . . she had the lights on and some candles lit as well."

"Maybe she's hiding a dead body?"

A burst of laughter stirred the group that was sprawled against the stone wall. Only Brito didn't laugh.

"Nothing like that! . . . It's that . . . I don't really know, I'm afraid to say . . . "

"To say what?"

"Something . . . but, honestly, I'm afraid."

"You really are a sissy!"

"Your mother!"

"Stop playing games! . . . Let it out now!"

Brito's revelation dismayed the gang. Distrustful eyes, half afraid, they stared at the window in the corner of the tenement. A taste for adventure and a tiny memory of tall tales left them dumbfounded. Blackie John, a full eight years, scratching his head, found a way:

"The best thing to do is to tell the folks inside!"

A rustling went through the house from end to end. Startled eyes were followed by a slamming of doors, by steps trampling down the halls. Those arriving from work kept swelling the wave of activity, and from the upstairs floor steps clattered down the stairwell. Lickety-split, almost ubiquitously, the kids raised the tenement into an uproar. The excited women took the lead in the midst of the wailing from some cradle suddenly abandoned. The men, curious, followed behind, amazed by the novelty of the situation. One skeptic or another scoffed in derision:

"There's no such thing!"

A stream of language in a strange dialect, a wailing lament, escaped from Ida's door. Her voice was fiery and strong, nobody had heard her like this, and it produced a lump in the throat of the crowd that was squeezing into the hallway. The suspicions increased. Rosa, of rugged hand and robust figure, struck her fist against the wood:

"Knock the door down!"

The palms of her hands covering her eyes and the kerchief on her head, Ida spurted out the prayer with her body swaying over the candles. Almost always she prayed in a low voice, her lips accelerated. Today, down deep, the cry of the prayer was a malediction and never before had her shoulders swayed so much. Today, Ida didn't beseech God, but with the same words, she yelled, offended. She neither sensed the noise nor the banging. The door was not completely shut and so it wasn't necessary to knock it down. Her heated voice, in measured pace, hadn't let her notice the crushing multitude that was filling up the room. In between her eyes and the palms of her hands, molded in the darkness, she envisioned the faces of Isaiah and her children, of Isaiah almost as a saint. When she lowered her arms, the multitude discovered her abundant tears. A silence left them immobile, and a sensation of uneasiness, discomfort, had dampened their spirits. Ida was a heap of nerves, slackened, without the strength to move her lips. She didn't even feel scared. A slight internal disturbance disclosed by a quiver of her head. Her wrinkled and weary face scanned the room. Her hands began to get ready for the mimicry and a furrow of supplication outlined itself on her mouth.

"Let's leave, my friends. It's nothing at all!"

A man's voice resounded, giving the signal to withdraw, and the squeaking of shoes through the doorway turned into a growing murmur outside the apartment.

"That's what prayer is over there in their country." The same voice. On the stairs going up to the next floor, the womenfolk milled around and Brito's mother gave him a beating:

"That will teach you to spy into other people's window, that'll teach you!"

Ida standing still before the candles, her eyes on the flames, didn't try to straighten out her thoughts. The crowd inside her room, suddenly like that, appeared vague to her, and she wouldn't know how to explain it. Friday. The first Friday in the tenement. From within came a feeling of rupture, of something that had been lost with the shouted prayer. The four whitewashed walls seemed strange to her and as she tried to bring her prayer to a close, the murmured words came to her mechanically. A tightening in her throat made her let out with a sob everything that was eating her up inside. She felt hollow. Her thin fingers intertwined and with her two fists fused together she rubbed her forehead. Hollow. She blew the candles out one at a time, serene, calm. Seated in front of the candlesticks, Ida's eyes stared at the extinguished wicks, and tracing the line of the drops of wax, globules heaped into strange miniatures, her head toppled silently on to the white tablecloth.

JUDITH

Gently. The breeze from the sea puffed the white curtains, stirring the fringes on the easy chairs. She sat down. The maid asked her to wait a few moments. On another occasion she'd sweep her eyes over the walls and the heavy furniture. She'd be amused by the little baroque figures cast in bad taste. She'd feel the soft wires of the springs give way under her weight, caving into a convex hump to make her comfortable. Today, impossible. She was afraid they would hear her heartbeat or that the heaving of her breasts would attract attention. Today she was all hesitation, she had created an outer shell, forcing her to hold back all gestures, a shell she now and then tried to crack in revolt. Her finger pressing the elevator's button had transmitted the energy needed to hold the door open. Now, crossing her feet, she seemed to have lost it completely. Torn toecaps on her shoes. Speckled with mud on the fold of the sole. Tremor. Lifting her foot off the carpet, she rested it on the waxed floor. The scene had been totally imagined. Last night her eyes glued to the ceiling (he had fallen asleep after much whining. The curtains enveloped his crib), she suppressed her tears in anticipation. Her sister. She would be the only one to whom she could turn. The others distanced themselves out of stubbornness, incomprehension. In bed, alone, she caressed his absent body by suffocating the pillow. Her sister. They were only a few years apart. Certainly she hadn't forgotten their mutual dreams shared by the window on rainy days, or the secrets they exchanged when going to sleep in their bedroom. In between two decorative plates, the photograph of their smiling parents, arm in arm, surprised her with its expression of comfort and protection. And she would have these benefits if in exchange she gave up everything else. Today she had nothing more to request. She heard that a period of mourning followed her departure, and that on the day of their marriage ceremony (only a civil one, as both of them had wisely agreed), there were cries and laments as though they were participating in the funeral procession of some corpse. Afterwards the silence that settles in and depresses. The solitude. The lack of communication. At night when he had taken her to the suburb, she knew a total break had taken place, and despite all the courage she had mustered, she couldn't suppress the bitter cry of one who, despite convictions, was at the same time harboring and violating a whole pile of emotions. Her sister. She was quite sure. Had always shared her ideas but just with greater reserve and a certain amount of hesitancy, especially when someone else would randomly touch upon them. But she did share them. Sometimes the cats disturbed her sleep with their running about and mating, and today more than ever, after much clawing, one of them had made her skin bristle with a wail that seemed more like a child's cry. The body spun around quickly, the head supported by the hand. The crib, motionless, curtained. Relief. She embraced her knees with her hands and let herself stay still with her eyes staring at nothing. It will be one month on the day after tomorrow since they brought his dead body home from the factory. (The bullet had hit his skull.) She had the child to her breast when the door opened and some men carried him to the bed, but it was all in vain. It will be one month on the day after tomorrow. She automatically pushed the hair from her eyes. She distinctly heard the buzzing, the tiny sounds piling up, consisting of strange dissonance to ears begging for silence. The little her friends could share had almost run dry. The inevitable day loomed with the reminder of hard times. On her nightstand, a sealed envelope with money set aside for the rent. Her other friends, their feelings deadened with time, were showing signs of impatience. And within her a cord clogging her larynx, wrapping around her tongue, and entangled in the crevices between teeth that became dreadfully obsessed in grinding together so that unknown things not escape. She would work. No doubt about it. She had never been frightened by such an idea. When she had decided to tie herself to someone who was not of her kind, she was perfectly conscious of her action, which in turn did not represent a total rejection of her roots (she had ingrained in her a whole way of life that a simple act or attitude does not displace), nor had he forced or demanded her to do such a thing. In that action there was a desire to outdo herself, something that transcends mere habit or custom. She knew it was difficult to understand. But once the step was taken, she considered herself clear of conscience and mature in her decision. Her hesitation was due to that life in the crib. And what about him? Two months and two days. His eyes certainly hadn't recorded his father's features, nor had the timber of his voice remained in his ears. He was completely isolated, without even roots that might be able to direct his life. Either his reddened face winced sleepily the whole day long, or his hands avidly groped for her breast. Her sister. Yes. Her sister. She had married. She had heard this through other sources, given her marginalized situation. She imagined the contrasts between her solitary room and a hypothetical apartment. Intruding eyes would see the shiny film foreshadowing her tear. She composed for herself an emotional scenario of an imaginary welcome. Her sister's thin face, her dreamy manner, she would glue her lips to that face, foreseeing their reunion. Her emotions were so overpowering they almost became a concrete presence. Her sister's thin face would be a welcoming bosom for her sobs. It's possible that a son would also be a concern of hers, she didn't know. If so, how easy it would be. To their already existing affinity another would be added which only feelings and not words could reproduce. She had vacillated. With difficulty she controlled her hesitancy, not out of pride, but fear. The reflection of the ficus on the window swayed back and forth, projecting deep inside ways of being that alternated with her breathing. The absence of her companion had opened gaps in her sense of security and assurance, where fleeting elements of doubt found easy access, as though attempting to undermine her. Now, there in the living room, her shoes crossed, her eyes transfixed on the expression of her parents, she was wavering and almost regretting the trip, the cradle entrusted to neighbors's hands. She didn't sense the smell of a child, a smell of washed diapers and talcum powder to which she had become so accustomed. Her sister would be pregnant. She imagined her like that. Large eyes. Thin face. Delicate hands hanging by her side. Her enormous womb a prediction. Through which door would she enter? A splash of oil in a frying pan made her think she would be coming from the kitchen with her apron. How would she react? She had told the maid she was merely an acquaintance, a friend.

"Judith?"

Terrifying vision of the visit's futility. Her intuition had given her the concrete certainty of an action taken in vain, of the act's gratuity. Neither the embrace, nor the kiss on the face, the thin face had been lost and had become rounded into features of affluence, her dreamy manner lost into an empty bloated expression. Not even the inflated womb but a general obesity that wasn't a prediction of anything. Her fatty hand had slipped like sausages between her fingers. Seated, they faced each other. In her eyes, yes, in her eyes a glow accidentally glimmered as the remembrance of dreams. But fleeting. Or nonexistent, who knows. Perhaps pure invention of her mind which forcibly sought to identify in the other the image she had been recomposing the whole night before. A hiatus. Perhaps both were searching for a thread that would reconnect them, but this was nonexistent. Slight ripple under her chin which rounded out even more her sister's inexpressive demeanor. Where were the special signs that distinguished her, where the gentle manner, exuding something fragile, sensitive? Curt were the sentences of exchanged information. Protocol. As for the rest, silence. Silence in relation to what had happened. Almost like two strangers in a doctor's or dentist's waiting room.

The whole charge of affection, about to burst, had withdrawn, repressed, due to something discouraging.

She risked asking a question.

Monosyllabic answer.

She remembered some neighbors.

They were doing fine, thank you.

She remembered the little boy from the house next door.

Both of them used to push his baby carriage. He was seven months old at the time.

He grew up. He moved. She didn't know where.

And their childhood friends?

Around, married.

And Julieta?

She had never seen her again.

Did she remember Maia, the old French teacher?

Yes.

She had bumped into him the other day.

Yes?

To what extent would she put up with that static behavior. She searched into her sister's eyes for something that would mean rejection, scorn, dislike. A sign that would tell her to retreat, the inconvenience of her being there. There was a deadening sense to her sister's feelings. With her gestures clipped, the only thing left was a stilled figure, without any volition.

Where did she live?

In the suburbs.

Far?

Yes.

Had she come by train?

Yes.

Horrible, all packed, isn't it?

Yes.

She felt her hairs stand on end and her goosebumps swell. In between the lines she sensed a vital awakening in her sister. For sure, some inhibition prevented her sister from hurting her full force. And in that moment she would have responded with everything. Everything. Her husband's death. Her son. She wanted so much to speak of her son. To describe his gestures, his manner. Why all this beating around the bush? Circumlocutions. Escape. Subterfuges. With her eyes she appealed for more intimate questions. Useless. She could continue to uphold the dialogue. What for? To ask her things already known or easy to discover intuitively. Her husband would be working. The apartment (where was the good taste of years ago?) gave her a sense of security. What else? The details are of little importance. At this hour would the neighbor be playing with her son? Or changing his diaper. Or shaking the rattle to stop his wailing. She squirmed in the easy chair. She saw her sister get up to answer the phone. She hadn't even heard the ringing. Outside a car honking its horn, a radio soap opera and some maid humming a samba. Once again her sister sat down. Did she want to have something to drink? No, thank you. (In the morning she had rushed out of the house. Had breast-fed her son and had forgotten to eat. Or she hadn't bothered.) She was already feeling the twinge of hunger rise from her stomach. Downstairs she would buy something, a piece of fruit.

"Daddy?"

If she had left sooner, she wouldn't have felt the disappointment of her unanswered question, the upset manner of one who had touched upon a taboo subject. No movement whatsoever on the part of her sister. Not even some distraction of pretending not to have heard. But head on. Her eyes on hers. She distinctly saw her image in her sister's pupil, despite the distance. The wrinkle on her chin had rippled like someone who swallows without water. She didn't want to hate, but the affective charge had passed from one pole to another. She hadn't destroyed the past. She was sure she had in front of her somebody who had lost her life. She had made a mistake. She had entered a place where time had stopped and where they would no longer understand her. Stagnation. The door closed after a cold farewell. Once again, like a sausage her sister's fatty fingers slipped through hers. Calling for the elevator she sensed a muffled sob from one about to burst out crying. Like a luminous sign the numbers followed each other in an on-and-off rhythm until they stopped. Her hand on the elevator doorknob, she waited, the final death-rattle, for the outburst that would confirm her mistake. The cicada was buzzing inside the elevator car. Somebody impatient was waiting for the elevator. She counted for a few seconds. She became absorbed with the almost simultaneous silence of the buzzing and her crying. Complete emptiness. In the descent a course had been set. Impossible to negate the past. However, she knew going back was also impossible. Tomorrow she would take her son to be circumcised. Moreover, she will know how to raise him so that he will remember his dead father and understand her. In being hit by the breeze, she felt a childish joy of one who discovers new worlds in an old shoebox, of one who, after mourning, rediscovers small happy details in the surrounding grey atmosphere. Now, the train. Her breast ready for him to dive into and suckle.

LITTLE GRINGO

He was crying. Not really out of fear of the possible spanking, despite his torn uniform. His mother wouldn't even have time for that. The most she would do is yell in the middle of her daily routine. He would take his clothes off; at the bottom of the wardrobe he would find his other outfit, soiled, for loafing around. Turning the corner, he was sure he would do nothing today. His feet, like alternating knives, cut into the mud from the rain. On the mango tree in the empty lot where they chased grasshoppers, or played ball, hung the rope from the improvised swing. He recognized it. It had been his and was what had remained of the heavy crate that his family had brought over. Nobody on the street. Surely the others had not come home from school or were they already having lunch. Nobody noticed his crying. The neighbor smiled as she scared the muddied cat off the easy chair on her porch. He held in his sobs as he pushed open the gate. He rubbed his face with his sleeve, leaving streaks of mud on his cheeks.

The leaves of the ficus tree were still shiny from the rain. He looked at the clinging vine. A young plant but it was already climbing almost past the window. In the living room, he hesitated between the kitchen and the bedroom. With a kerchief on her head, his mother would be peeling potatoes or grinding meat. He had caught her attention as he threw his books on the bureau. That he should go change his clothes and then fetch some onions at the grocery store. Nothing else. She hadn't even stuck her face in to notice his teary mood and his messed up clothes. As he entered his room, he was surprised by the babbling of his baby brother who, eyes to the ceiling, was playing an invisible harp. The room seemed strange to him, almost as strange as his friends, despite the months that had passed. His eyes on the blackboard, he squinted as if to help the sounds hampered by his tongue. Like a robot, he copied the names and numbers (these he understood), trying to figure out the teacher's sentences. Sometimes he would lose his place while staring at her. Her incisor teeth jutting out, her hair reminding him of hats worn by ancient mummies, her thick lips. Other times, he would roll his eyes over the walls that were covered with maps and pictures of big shots. The window reminded him of the street where he felt better. There he didn't have to talk much. Just listen. No written tests or oral exams. The nickname. The kids' constant pestering bothered him. He rubbed his swollen eyes in front of the mirror. Yesterday he rolled in the ditch with Caetano after an argument. He spoiled their game. In the urge to knock him down, the little black boy grew in size before his eyes.

"Dumb little gringo!"

He spread his uniform on the bed. He wouldn't do his lesson. To go back to the same school, he also knew that was impossible. If it were up to him, he wouldn't go to another one. Way back when, before the ship, he had his gang of friends. In the summertime, they used to meet in the square and crossing the field they'd reach the small creek, where they could dive in naked without fear. In compensation for the dullness of the lessons given by the bearded old geezer (whose wide and heavy hand was felt by his slaps and pinches) there was the forest. Chestnut trees of prickly fruit and ample shade, hills where a body could roll down to the edge of the road. Raspberries they picked to their hearts' content. Carrots stolen from the neighbor's garden. His mother's voice repeated the request for the onions. He unwittingly scratched his head. In the wintertime there was the sled that was carried up the river, the frozen river where his ironclad boots slid like skates. At home the hot soup of beets, or the steaming cabbage. He would sit on the lap of his grandfather who had just come from prayers and enthusiastically would repeat what he had learned in school. Where is grandfather? He used to like the scraping of the old man's beard on his neck, tickling him, and of the stories he would tell him at bedtime. Always about the miracles of saintly men. He would dream contentedly about eternity. His grandfather's voice was hoarse but good to listen to. Even more so when he sang. His eyes on the beamed ceiling or following the stove's chimney pipe, his melody would cut through his own sleep. Today he had arrived late. He didn't like to call attention to himself, but he had to go to the teacher's desk to explain the delay. Fifty pairs of eyes staring at his trembling feet. The request for the onions became more insistent. Massive laughter in counterpoint to the stammering of his mouth, eyes, and hands. With difficulty he withheld his tears as he took his place. He had cried like this on the first Saturday, when wearing his yamulka he went out with his father in the direction of the synagogue. Caetano, Raul, Zé Paulo, Betinho, at the end of the street chimed in unison repeating the refrain, *little gringo*. Looking at the hanging rattle, he came across his brother's eyes staring at his own. Goo-goo. A listless smile. He had sat down in his seat. He had opened the book to the designated page, groping like a blind man to get in step with the reading. He hadn't gotten used to either the historical figures or for him the strange stories which he read haltingly. *Speak up, little gringo.* Came the voice from the back, thick, like from someone older. *Speak up, little gringo.* It insisted. While turning his neck to discover the source he had been caught by the roll call order of the reading. He looked at the sharp teeth insinuating themselves on to the lower lip as if to escape. How to explain to her? How? Mute he lowered his head like a cat ashamed of having done some mischief. Tears were easy for him. He remembered one Sunday. He crossed the patio with Raul who had called him to come to his house. In the back of the cemented yard, under a covering, the two teams of tiddlywinks got ready. From the pantry still the noise of the utensils, end of the dinner meal. They called them. The mother cut the melon and separated two slices. Raul thanked her for both of them. "Oh! It's the little gringo!" With the smoke from the cigarette expelling through his nose, it was the father who had let loose the exclamation. The fruit in his mouth almost chokes him. The aunts and uncles concentrate their attention upon him. He felt like a shrunken creature, dejected, paralyzed, his two hands holding the slice in between his teeth. *"Speak up, little gringo!"* Chorus. *Speak up, little gringo.* Once again the voices behind his desk. That other time he had run like a cornered animal in the midst of the laughter. Nestled in his room and in his mother's lap, he got everything off his chest. Goo-goo. Shaking the rattle. A smell of urine awakens him from his sluggishness. A stream trickled from the diaper on to the rubber sheet. *Speak up, little gringo.* He felt himself recoil and fall backwards with the chair. In the midst of the shouting the old biddy's claw grabbed him in suspension, mussing up his shirt. Some of the kids were standing on the desks, and feeling surrounded he withdrew into expressive muteness. Of the intended vengeance the only thing that had remained was the frustration of not being able to explain, knowing it would be impossible. Goo-goo! The puddle of urine was beginning to bother him and after kicking his legs his baby brother burst into a drawling cry. Once again he shook the rattle, indifferently, with his eye on the street. The rattling had increased the baby's crying. He didn't notice his mother's entrance. Without looking at him she picked up his brother to rock him to sleep. She took the dry diaper from the drawer and in between lulling him to sleep and changing him, he calmed down. She persisted in her request from the grocery store. He tried to catch her attention, to win over the innocence he was entitled to. Afterwards he would like to fall into her lap, kiss her, and tell her everything, with the assurance of knowing he was right. But nothing like that happened. Gathering up the nickels he looked for the door. He would bring home the onions. And he wouldn't tell her that while he was being reprimanded in school, in his impotence to explain himself, when the old biddy began to smack the palm of his hand with the black plastic ruler, he couldn't contain himself and slugged her across the chest, tearing her dress. When he crossed the gate, he quickened his step spurred on by the will to become a man right then and there. He thought that by running he would speed up time. His feet skipped over the wet cement, like a long time ago when, with his ironclad boots, they slid across the frozen river in the wintertime.

DIALOGUE

Face to face. The distant whistle of the locomotive and the almost inaudible hiss of the hot water tank boiling; the cussing from the corner resounds down the street and is repeated by the neighborhood kids hanging around the lamppost; night which seems more like day, clear, an almost bluish blackness above the horizon of the hill and the edges of the tiled rooftops. Separating them, merely the width of a room and the dense fog of countless cigarettes. Seated next to a low cabinet, the father rests his arm on top and settles his head in the palm of his hand. When the son had entered, he was already there, with the same stance, devising arguments for some expected confrontation, recomposing and reelaborating suspicions which indicated the need for urgent action. With the cigarette between his teeth, the son avoided the greeting that would cause a break in his thoughts, a momentary suspension in the crystallization of his ideas, which for him, ill accustomed to decisions, would be a disaster. He had heard the toilet flush in the bathroom and, after, the noise of the utensils in the kitchen. The tap water dripping in the sink, the rattling of a pan cover on the stove, the vegetable taste of the soup splaying with steam as it fell into the soup plate. He became irritated with the statement made by the maid who was in the pantry. Noises never bothered him, words did. Accustomed to a muteness from which he sometimes tried to free himself without success, he felt compensated by his own awareness of the tiny imbalances in his silence. His pondering did not change, since he never got to the bottom of his thoughts, suffice it for him the simple chain of ideas within a very restricted cycle of constant brooding. With words his reaction was the opposite. He became inarticulate. He lost control. He was filled with the vague notion of an understanding, of an awareness, but in no way would it affect him. Almost always unintelligible, he saw words as lost elements, impossible fragments of some future conversation. Those that bore vestiges of tenderness needled him even more for his never having savored their taste. And it wasn't just a few times when, yelling at the top of his voice, he had driven away lovestruck couples who preferred the shadows of the property's iron-grated fence and the immense lampshade of the almond tree with its slanted trunk expelling branches that stretched out over the curbstone. What did the maid have to say to him. That she served dinner and that was that! Moving sideways he had passed through to the pantry and, in a fraction of a second, had parked into his bent position over the table. His stomach contracted, and he held the spoon in the bottom of the soup plate as he felt himself being watched. He knew he was being observed and the interference hindered his movements. He crumbled the bread, molding small spheres with his nervous fingers. Discontent, he flattened them with a willful brusqueness. Relief. An imponderable but assured notion that he was the master of his space. The spoon's movement had generated a current on the green and golden surface, breaking through the thick transparency of iridescent speckles. Why alter the state of things with a sudden decision? Now the stretched arm serving the shallow platter. Rice, eggs, round slices of tomato, slimy slices of roast from the red-hot olive oil that was still crackling in the frying pan. The question about his appetite veers his chaste attention away from the outline of her rump, gracefully sloping up to her ample waist. Vulgar urges that a deep-rooted modesty was forcing him to bury. That he once and for all break with the impossible, any kind of foolish act, a hullabaloo, and to gain at least the satisfaction of establishing a precedent to hold on to for future attempts! Nauseous presence of garlic in the meat shredded by the fork. How much time would it take to eat it? In getting up from the table, no other alternative would be left to him except the easy chair facing his father, and all the rest.

Face to face. At last, the hope of the day had plunged headlong, and the moment became somber with the thickening of the smoke. His attention on the thumb, and the index finger that rubs an excess of skin against the fingernail. That I-need-to-talk-to-you, voiced yesterday with a new emphasis, brought to mind a potential succession of hypotheses. And what he most feared was the decision he felt capable of making if pushed to the extreme, as well as the urge to make possible a final break gush forth from within. He wanted to avoid it. He accrued arguments for small personal clashes and managed to postpone it. Where would they get to today? On the bus going downtown he predicted the oscillation of feelings that would alternate until nighttime. He became irritated with the bus's jolts and by his side the kicking of the kid in the mother's lap. The façades of the row houses seemed ugly to him, the petty and dirty commerce of small shops, or the garish, imbecilic overabundance of formica and signs. The cannibalism of the butcher who, right by the bus stop, was shattering ribs on the wooden block, brandishing his short-handled meat cleaver, with blood splattering his face and his apron streaked with clots. A truck's maneuver, two cars crossed in front of the trolley, and in the distance a little red flag and the trembling of a rock crusher. And in the same locale. Chickens bald and impaled, torn quarters of bleeding steers on hooks, and the lunar pallor of suckling pigs in the cooler's showcase. A blue strip of morning sky suggested calmness and reconciliation, anticipating quietude and a restful appreciation of the landscape. However, it would only take one word, an indiscreet gesture gone astray, to spoil his enthusiasm. He attended class, drifting between a rush of attention and prolonged remoteness where he felt entirely alien to the locale, portraying himself through the habits and desires of others. From the window a curve of beach, solace, a hypothetical representation of comfort, an absence of drama in the succession of waves. At work as well, intermittent enthusiasm and brooding. Annoyed with the cuff of his shirt sleeve that gets wet in the lavatory, with the sportcoat that shows the pleats from ironing, and not the softness of linen, getting annoyed with the skin that covers a body with the same roughness as crude cotton.

Face to face.

His father's head sways, unglues itself from his hand and falls slightly forward. Eyes staring into eyes. After all, imbecile, what do you want? Those books of yours what did they teach you? I'd like to use another type of language with you if you didn't take on that presumptuous and headstrong air. Cretin, take a good look at me! Do you think I'll show you the road to perdition or misfortune? Look around and see the asininity of your obstinacy, think reasonably but without the stubbornness of the jackass.

His fingers tremble, they bring the cigarette close to his mouth without altering his position.

In an automatic gesture, the son imitates him, and with this in-sult his eyelids contract. Even if I could speak to you frankly, what good would it do? Is it presumptuous of me to know that you cannot understand me, in spite of your intention? Or that you would under-stand me, if I were someone else, as you want me to be? If at times I express with irritation, and merely with my look, terms such as the ones you could be hearing now, can't you see that I'll regret it right away? And why? Because it hurts me to know that you could not deal with me in any other way, because it's your nature, from all that stuff they inculcated in you, and which you didn't get to inculcate in me.

He expels the smoke. Resists clearing his throat. Imbecile! Imbe-cile! You think you're more wise because I let go of the reins. But pay attention! Just what is it that I cannot understand about you? The fact of my not agreeing with the way you are facing the future? With the life you intend to lead? Answer me then, wiseguy, what is life if not this, a search for solidity, for security, a guarantee not only for to-morrow, but for the week, the month, the year? And to this you fight me with empty words!

The cussing still echoes outside on the street, like the uproar from the street urchins amidst the hissing sound of the locomotive. For an instant his head lowers into what could be taken as a pause, but again it straightens up and the gaze is fixed. Can't you see that it's impos-sible? Empty words. Empty words. But not empty for me, do you hear? There exists between us the atrocious distance that can't be mea-sured in years or kinship, distance for which you probably consider yourself guilty, yes, you let go of the reins, but now you're implacable.

The eyebrows funnel into the furrow on his forehead. I agree. But what has this got to do with life? What does it have to do with it?

In contention his teeth bite his lower lip. Can't you see that a simple question doesn't put me at ease? That by itself, it is an acknowledgment of this disconnectedness. Could you by chance understand that not everybody takes pleasure in this routine of procreating and getting fat, in addition to the vile stigma of imbecility that brands stone faces into an enduring delusion? Would it be possible for you to conceive (and I don't believe so, since centuries have stratified your emotional state, reducing it to a formula only defied by instinctive impulses), would it be possible for you to conceive of the grotesque, the sublime, the sordid which can in the fraction of a second pass through the soul? And with that intensity of perception goes a whole preparatory state, sometimes involving rejection. Can't you see it is precisely the way one reacts to that moment that determines the choice one makes for a certain existence?

His eyebrows contract a little, but soon relax. In his dilated pupil, the reflection of someone who is always waiting. Hollow words, not mute ones. And these are the arguments you give to explain your madness! Imbeciles, the others, but you, of course not? Is there anybody stopping you from thinking, denying you the right to everything you keep on boasting about as being the essence of things? Think the way you want, but act, with your head and your feet on the ground. Were the occasion otherwise, I would tell you a fable, but you have the gift of going so far as to invert the meaning of any one of them.

He is bothered by the image in those paternal eyes, staring back at him with a fixity not intended for him, bullet that ricochets. Were the occasion otherwise, I would also tell you a fable. But if I had to speak now, I would tell you that all this business is perhaps rebellion and in your favor, even if you don't see it. Rebellion against what was not a stigma, but ended up by being so, and from this vicious cycle nobody tries to get out. Security. Stability. What good were these when they ganged up against us (and this us is still a little of what you gave me) and nothing came of it but death. What good were the imprecations . . . or the prayers? And what victory was there?

He recoiled in the easy chair, seeing the body of the old man standing, agile as he had not seen him for some time, leaning half forward, his arm insinuating a slap. He knew his fear did not derive from the intended blow, but from the reaction to what had not even been said. Animal reflex, he had raised one of his legs and the palm of his hand spread out, protecting his face. He hated himself for not managing to stay calm, and right then and there, at least, to put his ideas in some order. But all of them. Every single one. And to think about them, despite the violence, despite the possibility of seeing them transmitted into another language not made of words. To think about this language without smoothing its edges, coarse words, with their angular contours and entangled brambles, and their edges sharper than a knife's. And instead, not to stand there, stupid, a frightened beast withdrawing its paws and snout. What air holds up the weight of this hand that does not fall? What energy shores up this blow that does not come? A feeling of discomfort, expecting the dinner to rise in his chest in the form of vomit. Moreover, only tension manages to keep him vacillating without coming to some closure. Let the arm fall and he'll have the chance to react. Fleeing to some corner with the childish taste of fear. The wild madness of blocking the blow with another, taking part in the demented and irrational fury. The acidic paste emerges in his mouth and forms around the edges of his teeth. He stirs it with his tongue and, disgusted, ingests it again. Perhaps he needs to talk. And he doesn't want trouble. Contractions in his stomach. Dizziness. The tear rolls down, not out of lament, but expelled by the pressure in his eyes. And with that gesture he had conveyed his intended meaning. His arms stretched out in space and a cold steel posture holding up the rest, compressing, distending, and relaxing his muscles without movement, yet nullifying his balance. The locomotive's whistle was now strident, and even clearer was the gush of steam expelled from its piston. Sudden silence after the obscene chorus of words on the sidewalk. An acrid odor of green almond within the window's rectangular space, and the rustling tremor of the big leaf branches. The same breeze brings the muddy smell of the water in the ditch, the rebellious shriek of the goaded parrot, the song of lament from the flute on the radio, and a flavor of hot bread, the bakery's last batch. The father's hand descends calmly and sways limply against his thigh. The son's body follows it as it returns to its normal position. The shoe firmly placed again on the wooden floor, the arm rubbing against the upholstered chair. The old man sits down but his face displays a sorrowful bitterness, he lights up a cigarette, rests his elbow on the cabinet, and his head upon the closed fist. But there are no reflections in his pupils. He had lowered his eyelids.

Face to face.

CHRISTMAS WITHOUT CHRIST

Tear a man away from his peace, his silence, his routine of cutting a slice of meat or taking a sip of ordinary wine on an extraordinary day, raise his criminal face stigmatized by who knows what habits, leave his body exposed inside-out in visceral nudity, a new buffoon fondled by the scourge of bruising caresses, chase the simian tail in his coccyx, chop off his ankles and in a burst of laughter split his capric skull, block his scintillating and ubiquitous eyes, root out his generating mass of ideas, conflicts, and sometimes feelings, amputate his sex and offer half to each one of the two mouths that stare at him with obscene grins, and from the ashes of his bones consumed by an unjust holocaust no vestiges are allowed, neither in the air, nor on the land, nor in the water, nor in the fire which precipitated them, nor in the remembrance of the one whose bones made these ashes. But then where to disperse them, where, if beyond the infinite there is another much bigger infinite? Thoughts? A speech made enthusiastically by the half drunk who suddenly recuperates his clear-headedness? He wouldn't know how to articulate it. Only the surge of feelings as a re-action to what he had heard, and the figure of Nani in front of him, at the head of the table opposite him, the glass of wine held by tremu-lous and wrinkled hands, the head of an old woman connected to black shoulders of silk, her wrinkles stirred by a ravenous decrepi-tude, her rumpled complexion in the half-shadows of candles and the dim lights of the wall fixtures, her greedy fixation upon the amount of wine allowed. It is Nani who becomes the object of Nehemiah's, Nehemiah Goldenberg's gaze, while the others go on chatting as if nothing there had changed, and it is in Nani that he tries to catch a glimmer of support, some approval, if there is approval, a response, if one is forthcoming. It is Nani, remote, doting, alien to any logic what-soever, fixated on the wine, seeking unconsciously to revive emotions, to warm nerves of buried dreams, but yet still dominating the table completely, it is in Nani that he wants to catch her total hatred, with-out subterfuges, within the truthfulness of her dementia. From what is now being said and from what will soon be said, he will not retain one word. His intention is the opposite. To retrace everything. To re-store the sentences he heard the instant they were pronounced, and to reweigh them within their static context, without the usual con-nectives, without the purpose of communication. It is in Nani that he seeks to stop time, to stop it until it becomes immobile, so that, once inertia is surmounted, he will be able to invert the flow of time. Never to go against the current, but to contain its impetus, to subdue it, and to turn its course upstream. They were talking about Jews dur-ing that Christmas supper when Nehemiah, at first feeling constrained, was overcome by his sudden awareness of being the intruder invited there by his friend, and even more brusquely came the other conclu-sion: there was the whole universe, the others and he, experiencing the same clichés, and the same unsolvable contradiction. Only Nani had asked for more wine. Nani, Ana Castanheira de Miranda Campos, with her seventy-five years of physical energy ruling over her ten subjects at that far end of the dining room of a modern residence, with its grey and blue walls, its motley easy chairs, its anatomical benches, its amoeba-like vases, its immense picture window with its low sill overlooking the Bay of Urca, the mountainous crests and the reflection in the calm waters of the bay, and the contrast between the meter-and-a-half pine tree, already divested of the holiday gifts, and a baroque Christ halfway up the wide mural on the wall facing Nehemiah, in back of Nani. They were talking about Jews during that Christmas supper, near the multicolored pine tree and facing the Christ eternalized in the spasm of his last terrestrial pain. And there they were to Nehemiah's left: Albino Fontoura, Nani's son-in-law, importer and representative of various state industries; Lenita, a brunette sportswoman of seventeen, green inconsequential eyes, daughter of Albino; another son, already married, Luís (a successful politician on his very first election, a vest adjusting a roly-poly body, temples and forehead radiating an eternal calmness), and his wife, Vera, daughter of a career senator, a thin, angular, and melancholy face, straw hair, a slender neck boxed in the two burrows of her small décolletage; Sílvio, brother of Lenita and Luís, Nehemiah's friend, and fellow teacher in the same junior high school, a neutral face, brown hair always in place, timid, self-absorbed. To the right: Mrs. Miranda Campos Fontoura, Nani's daughter, fifty-five years of calmness in the apathy of a not-too-aged face, of successful childbirths, of serene emotions, with an indefinite glow of one who always wanted to operate on the outside but who never thought of taking a step toward the door; Eneas, her son, and Albino, her oldest, the thirty-five spry and victorious years of a prosperous lawyer with a lucrative practice of abundant lawsuits, and his wife, Malu, Marta Cavalcante Fontoura, a placid, domestic expression as she reclines her head, a woman who only asks for a pillow or a kiss in order to fall into an indifferent sleep; Labieno de Miranda Campos, another of Nani's sons, suspiciously forty, a deliberate and serious voice, but somewhat satiny, teeming with emphatic modulations, a critic of the plastic arts and the secretary of a professional magazine, almost bald, manifesting obesity in his rounded chin and gestures, one who spends the day walking on thick rugs; Vânia Fontoura, sister of Albino, forty years old, dirty blond hair, skin from the indolence of sunbathing at the beach, legally separated, pretty, uninhibited. Facing him, Nani, with her wine glass between her fingers and her lips drawn back in the anticipation of pleasure. And he, Nehemiah Goldenberg, thirty complex and troubled years, history teacher, nonconformist, restless, bearing in his actions the despair of obscure causes and the serenity of those already lost; neither light nor dark hair, two eyes, a forehead, a nose (an illusion, the straight and classic line from the bridge of his eyebrows down to his lip?), a mouth, a face, two hands, two legs, a torso, and a chest, and a member in his groin. By dint of constant abstractions, Nehemiah had already immobilized all of them even though nothing at the table reflected the process of capturing their previous state. Amidst hands that spread, that criss-cross knives and forks, that lift greenish glasses, or that dab the napkin on their lips—here is the static group of his design. His own organism keenly feels a bit of the effort squandered, inasmuch as he had not deprived himself of drink, but his determination infuses him with vital juices and internal stimulants, enlivening his arteries and muscles, leveling two tensions. His left hand holds the fork, his right hand stopped the cutting of the knife and let the blade stay carved in the slice of pork roast. And acknowledging his impulse, he is ready to go ahead with the inversion of the facts, with the capture of lost fluxes, with the reconquest of one instant, that alone will make it possible for him to weigh cumulative arguments.

"Jews are very charming, very charming. And an extraordinary political sense. Marx and Rothschild, Disraeli, and Bernard Baruch . . . An extraordinary political sense. They have the world in their hands." In the mouth that now chews, in the juxtaposed lips, oscillating in the periodic contact with molars, Nehemiah reviews the primitive expression and rethinks Luis's eloquent gesture. The ceremonious tone, the clearly articulated sentence, the vacuity of the traditional resources (is this how nations govern themselves?), the "high falutin" use of tongue-twisting names, that's the level of comprehension. The smooth caress with the taste of an ironic slap but which, at the moment for decisions or for positions in jeopardy, will come crashing down like a harsh blow.

"Great financiers, entrepreneurs!" In what lucrative ventures were they useful to you, or in what swindles did you manage to outwit them? If by chance, Albino, if by chance you one day suffer a setback in that game which is the same for you as it is for them, and if by chance one of them benefits from your loss, somebody always benefits, will you say the same thing? Or will you look deep down, or not even so far, for the crudest expression, the clear-cut, decisive invective with the implication of a final verdict without appeal.

"And what shrewdness? Admirable!" To what shrewdness are you referring, Eneas, to the one most familiar to you, to the one you practice on a daily basis, by offering an eternal subversion of facts, ideas, concepts, proofs, to the one you manage, under the impact of well-planned rhetoric, to obfuscate the truth of some mistake, without the need for any metaphysical speculation as to whether or not to own up to this truth, to the one which by artful means eliminates the evidence, to the one that brings tears to your eyes in proportionate abundance according to your revenue or to your reputation, to the shrewdness that creates doubt, and from this doubt you extract the yes or the no, according to your interests, to the shrewdness that draws adequate subtleties from these bulky treatises that decorate your shelves, to the one which, in the name of some ethic or logic, represents the negation of these; is it to that shrewdness, Eneas, you are referring?

"But weren't the Jews the ones who killed Christ, Papa?"

Lenita was not able to repress the question which for her externalizes the unpleasantness of that presence; she manifests her reaction of antipathy that is caused by who knows what. Something in his eyes, in his mouth, in the movements of his hands, in the awkwardness of his helping himself to the food, in the lack of assurance with which he lifts the platter or fills his glass. She had already seen him several times in discussion with Sílvio, and she was turned off by her brother's subservience, always agreeing, incapable of offering opposing arguments that wouldn't be demolished by four or five harsh, cutting remarks; so in her head she mulls over thoughts in search of one that appears to her to be decisive. And what surfaced was the summary of millennia, the gross but effective crystallization of so many doctrinaire philosophies. The embarrassment causes a brief hiatus in the conversation. Everyone bent forward awaiting some aside, some gesture that would serve as pretext to make the response magically disappear. And the yes or the no answer could be said by anyone of them, even by him, Nehemiah. Would it be worth it? Atavistic reminiscences of frightful feelings befall him as he contemplates the Holy Week procession of the old country. The day condensed into hatred, the idea made into word, yes, and action. Perverse alchemy, intending to redeem the body while showing the claws that *all of us* have already clenched at one time. And in that phrase all theological arguments end, there the consequence of piles of ethical propositions is summed up, there the greatest soritical logic comes to a close: blood.

"And what works of genius did his death not inspire. Michelangelo, Rouault . . . "

Ironic or evasive? The smooth tone of the sentence fills the atmosphere heavily with tinges of hidden sordidness. Labieno stares at Nehemiah as if expecting some gesture of gratitude for the finesse used to get around the sudden silence. Laughter and the clinking of silverware attest to their relief at the somewhat improper but spirituous "out." Nehemiah looks straight at Labieno and confronts him with his undisclosed intention. The crease in his lips maintains the half-concealed smile, full of implied meanings that did not escape the other man's thoughts. Hence the greater repulsion. Names thrown out like that, under what pretext? He didn't want to go around generalizing, but for some time he was already bothered by those names, or similar ones, stated with nervous ecstasy. More than representing enthusiasm he saw the shell of erudition covering the same identical end: sordid and brutish. Crazy mannerisms in the face of a phenomenon that didn't go below the epidermis; feverish agitation without the true feeling of solemn emotions, without the stroke of drama felt in the most audacious attempt; merely an external vibration to mask a marginal, sterile, cynical, hardly ambiguous, plan. Useless to debate his theory when the other's face becomes blank and Labieno's hand presses the napkin to his mouth.

"Mister Nehemiah, you don't even seem Jewish. You enjoyed the roast pork so much." Malu smiled at him with the indulgence of one who comes to the aid of the needy, while Eneas approves of his wife's good sense in what he would call a *tactful move*, inspiring the stranger's admiration. But the smile disappears when in Nehemiah's expression there is no perceived reception for the praise. A bit more polished, and he would have made some gesture of gratitude. But the assumption about the ethos of those people coming-from-who-knows-where takes away the pleasure of being so courteous. Anything else would not be expected.

"Oh, . . . Oh, Mister Nehemiah, you've become broad-minded, isn't that so? The essential thing is being true to one's spirit, faith . . . tradition."

On another occasion he would have answered her with different gestures and, with different feelings, he would see her beautiful profile, her sunburnt skin, her tender eyes, the vertical line of her neck, and the natural curve of her shoulders. Her hair radiating natural high-lights, her mouth a little wide, slightly aggressive, but sincere in the modulation of hidden conformities. And in an undertone, he could whisper to her an affectionate "nonsense." Urges and words still lin-gered inside him. However, why bother now? Vânia emerged amidst the ordinariness of clichés, automatic affection in a dimly lit bar, her three daily thoughts mulled over and over prior to floundering in some corner. He felt her momentary interest. There was something exotic about him, a variant amidst the monotony of identical types. He noticed her graceful way of placing her hair at the back of her neck and her hand resting gently near his. He controlled himself.

"A little more wine, my daughter!"

Nani was asking for wine. It is Nani who becomes the object of Nehemiah's gaze while the others continue to chat as if nothing there had changed, it is in Nani that he tries to incite a spark of support, some approval, if there is approval, a response, if one is forthcoming. It is Nani, remote, doting, alien to any logic whatsoever, fixated on the wine, seeking unconsciously to revive emotions, to warm nerves of buried dreams, but yet still dominating the table completely, it is in Nani that he wants to unleash total hatred, without subterfuges, within the truthfulness of her dementia. In her he sees the historical continuity that doesn't acknowledge any form of adaptation, that consciousness already formulated, inflexible, not making room for readjustments or doubts, insensitive to the most concrete sign of her failure because she possesses the absolute truth. There exist in her fingers reminiscences of medieval intolerance and the determination of the most rigid of contemporary politics, there exists in her thumb the impulse of tetrarchs facing the vanquished lying in the arena. Nehemiah knows that words will mean nothing when the thumb is turned upside down. And Nani sips her wine.

On the wall the crucifix. The half-opened eyes, a serene shadow under the eyelids, the lips almost closed. The arms and the legs stretched and nailed to the cross. The shriveled belly, furrows along the line of the hips, and the hard muscularity of the thighs. Nehemiah looks at the long hair covering the forehead, the curly beard split into scrolls in the middle of the chin.

Would the answer come from you? Human or divine, you die repeatedly for our lives, and we always die your death. Your greatest apostle had an inkling of the eternal symbiosis, when, wanting to justify and save us, perhaps, planted the seed of our degradation in our simple presence as witnesses and pawns at the moment of global forgiveness. You and I live perpetual death and resurrection throughout the centuries. When your most dedicated servants, and even more dedicated are they to other inspirations, strive to do the best in their zeal: we die. When others more gentle, whose tenderness does not shun the hyena or the criminal, receive us with benevolence: we live as marginals, hated and feared, even though in our hand no other weapon is left except the last coin of some booty stamped and approved by somebody who gave it in your name. Prophet, they extracted from you the quintessence of your world vision, and with it forged the greatest era of exuberant thought: the Middle Ages. But of your life, they kept the moment in which you now exist: agony. Based upon your agony they staked out the universe and wove banners in its name, and when the ire of so many crowns begged for a palliative, there we were. And why are we to blame, if when they seek you out in your most simple form, in your earliest belief, they always find us? If Jeremiah's lament anteceded the Sermon on the Mount, if Amos's indictment preceded the response to the rights of Caesar? And afterwards came the new belief, and even those who no longer remember that agony, upon seeing us, remember that many times that's why we die: and so they kill us. And from this age-old confusion, procreated over a thousand years, when will we be released, you and I?

Sílvio serves him a little more wine. Nehemiah thanks him, turning his attention to his plate. He drives the knife in, cuts the slice and bites into it, followed by a swig of wine. Facing him, Nani gulps the glass down and stretches out her authoritarian arm.

"A little more wine! Today is Christmas!"

PARABLE ON THE SON
AND THE FABLE

And there he was, in bed, eyes wide open after his delirium. Flanking the bedside, the thin body and nervous face of his mother, and the shrunken outline of his father, both seated on small green upholstered benches, and each with a hand on the top sheet. A serene light was coming from the backyard, through the open window, the gentle three o'clock light of a sunny afternoon, and a sky washed by other days of rain, a clarity without noise, impregnated by a languor spreading over the neighborhoods, densely filled with sluggishness and free of any movement from branches or breezes. It is this light that the son's eyes, very wide open, aim for on the white ceiling, with no intention of moving, and guessing that there on the outside the color of an unblemished horizon was blue, albeit not in sight. The heat under the sheet does not bother him; on the contrary, it gives him a feeling of temporary comfort and well-being that he would like to see prolonged if they continued with their silence without the intrusion of words, even though he knew that these would not be delayed in coming, since the other two people were simply there for that reason, and in a few moments they would begin a supposed dialogue. The pile of mistakes had brought him to that jumbled state of madness and lucidity, and if he was there, in bed, with his eyes wide open after the delirium, and not in another place, dead, perhaps, above everything else, he owed it to an illusive perseverance in remaining there till now. But don't let them come to him with words for he expected nothing from these, because in his obstinacy he always heard and read them backwards, he, a mirror, and in the face of the others' astonishment, he marveled at how they didn't understand at all. At the time when he still believed in myths, he had shown signs of being unaware of boundaries. One time he looked at the fire and tried to bend the flame with the palm of his hand. He had screamed. But once the pain was gone, he persisted. So they punished him. If he didn't repeat the act, it wasn't due to the pain but rather to the humiliation of the punishment which in some vague way he intuitively understood. But they had never told him that within the color of the flame there existed pain. During the period when he still believed in fables, he had shown disrespect for boundaries. With a stick he tried to disenchant the house cat, and since it insisted in keeping its usual demeanor, pushing away with its paw the point of the stick he kept putting into its face, purring and opening its mouth wide, ready for some fun, he became furious and began to violently whack the animal. Having forgotten about past expressions of affection, and also not thinking to flee, the pet lunged at its loyal friend and left him all bloody. So they punished him. If he did not persist in this feat, it wasn't due to the blood or the tears, but to the same motive of humiliation as before, by now more clear to him. But they had never told him that cats knew nothing about fables. And now there he was, in bed, with his eyes wide open after his delirium.

"Son, I am going to tell you a fable," it was his mother's voice, almost faint. "When winter arrived and everything was snow and ice, the cicada, who had spent the whole summer singing, felt hungry. So he looked for the ant who during the good weather did nothing else but save and save food for the winter months, and he asked for a bit of that food to satisfy his hunger. However, the ant asked him: "And during the summer what did you do?!" "I sang, always sang, always," answered the cicada. "Well, go on and dance a jig now!" said the ant and shut the door in his face."

"But if the cicada acts like the ant, who will sing during the summer?"

"Son, I am going to tell you a fable," it was his father's voice, by now a little aggressive. "When the plague raged among the animals, the lion, convinced it was due to the sins there committed, called an assembly so that each one could confess, and the guiltiest would then die. He himself confessed the unjust deaths he caused, but the assembly forgave him. The same was done with the bear, the tiger, the leopard, and the wolf. The assembly forgave all of them. For it wasn't a sin to kill, to steal, to tear to pieces, to wound in a cowardly manner. And then came the donkey, and he said that while being hungry in the meadow of a convent, he could not resist and so he tasted the grass. And the assembly in full force, horrified by such a great calamity, roared, howled, barked, demanding punishment. And so the donkey was sacrificed."

"Father, I admire that donkey!"

"Son, I am going to tell you a fable," it was his mother's voice, by now almost in tears. "A shepherd was sleeping, heedlessly, and in the distance his dogs were guarding the flock. On to this scene approaches a serpent, and is ready to bite him, when a mosquito, who was also there, discovers that only one way to save the shepherd is to sting him. Waking up, the shepherd still had time to take hold of his staff and to smash the serpent's head. But the bite on his forehead was hurting him, and bothered by the mosquito, he lets his hand fall violently on top of it ."

"Mother, I have already been that mosquito!"

And his mother's head bends down in sobs. And in the torpor of the afternoon, in the serenity of a desired silence, only the grave and hoarse voice of the father can be heard:

"Son, if you want to live, forget about fables!"

THE SEVEN DREAMS

At that precise moment his world became the seventh dream of that Thursday in October. Seated in a wicker chair in the corner of the veranda, he was looking at the field behind the house and was fixing his eyes particularly upon the waterwheel's tile-covered shed. He was fully conscious of what was happening to him and even in that unusual situation he did not forget the chain of dreams that had taken him to the wicker chair in the corner of the veranda where he was looking at the field behind the house and was fixing his eyes particularly upon the waterwheel's tile-covered shed. It was sunny and everything indicated his just having finished lunch. In front of him a glass on the floorboards must have been used by him just moments before he recomposed himself inside the greater reality he intuited to be the last, as though he were lacking strength, or there was no need any more to prolong the chain of dreams. He had attained a sense of fullness never before imagined and he was fixing his eyes particularly upon the waterwheel's tile-covered shed with the inherent decision to move the cycle backward, hauling back to the previous stages some idea that would allow him at least to formulate the problem that had been posed at the start. Foolhardy when one doesn't suddenly perceive the concrete reality of each stage and goes on accepting the suggestion of any fantasy or symbol. At that precise moment his world became the seventh dream of that Thursday in October. Seated in a wicker chair in the corner of the veranda he was looking at the field behind the house and was fixing his eyes particularly upon the waterwheel's tile-covered shed. He got up, left the veranda, bypassed the trees lining the road, and walked toward the waterwheel. As he was kneeling next to the set of gears which drove the grindstone, he woke up in the sixth dream. In the exact same position he had fallen asleep to dream the waterwheel. The chair swayed a little and the metallic tower imposed itself with its interlace of beams. And the ethereal dawn was between gray and hazy blue. The row of low houses hadn't yet been disturbed by the rooster's crow and the poles that made up the railing of the veranda sliced his view of the tiled roof. He surrendered to the rocking of the chair with a voluptuous pleasure that only the dream allowed. The delicate frame, with slightly rounded corners, rocked resiliently, and the seat and the chairback's interwoven straw made his body experience a lightness equal to its weight or the strain on the chair. And while the light invaded the room and the roosters began again their defiant singing, he attempted in that oneiric return to discern the portion of the dream previous to his search. The question intrigued him even more because in the sixth dream, already back by now, he had a sketch of the last one and the recollection of the previous five. It was necessary to go back to the dream in which he was dreaming about some positive outcome. And the only thing positive was the impossibility of finding out about the gears of the grindstone and the impetus that now moved the rocking chair. Suddenly he got up as if something very important had been forgotten and the effort spent in this movement disturbed his sleep. He had gone back to the fifth dream. And the return was even more painful than the departure that had taken him to the sixth. Precisely because he was returning. The room in shadows, the upholstered easy chair in the middle and situated along the wider side of the room the carpet and the same guy in front of him. His repugnance had attained such an intense degree that only the dream, the sixth, removed him from the heaviness of deep sleep which he found to be an escape from the results of an uncontrollable coprophilic urge. The guy persisted in the same maneuvers made prior to his return. At first, and this was still before getting to the rocking chair and to the waterwheel, he seemed to hear him distinctly. He didn't exactly know what he had to tell him. He only knew that the other one seemed to hear him distinctly, even though at times he let a little laugh slip out, more a result of his lack of control than strictly motivated by something he might have said. In spite of that, he didn't remember if he had said something. The guy, short and fat with a roundish face, wavy hair combed upward and avid eyes hiding behind dark lenses, badly disguising a burning desire greater than his own, the guy suddenly left the other easy chair and threw himself at his feet. He felt the guy's fingers searching for his thighs and his hands dove avidly into the opening of his fly and eagerly enveloped his member. The surprise and the excitement hindered any reaction on his part. And moments later the guy's head was exerting pressure against his groin, and he only saw the undulating movement of his hair while a sucking action disabled something in him, he still didn't know exactly what it was. Now he saw the smiling face in front of him, a chubby face in between infantile and imbecile, and he tried to restrain a more violent urge by distracting himself with thoughts of a waterwheel's gears and a rocking chair of curved wood and the seat and chairback of braided straw. An irresistible impulse to move made him leave aside some coexisting contradictory thoughts and he landed a violent blow with his knee on the guy's mouth. The movement of his joints disturbed his sleep as well as the dream, which was the fourth, and he leaned his head against the marble sill of the louvered window that lit the room like primitive stained glass. He had finished his work, an indistinct group of people were having a dialogue near the head of a long table but no sound reached him. As though a vacuum were separating him from any word or sound. The heat must have been intense. His shirt wet, the knot of his tie irritating, his collar was up tight, too tight, the sweat dripping down his thighs and running down his legs. His throat dry, his tongue rough, he looked at the ornate top of the wardrobe in the middle of the back wall. Two circular arches crowned three vertical lines in perfect harmony and suggested the outline of an arcade. Against a blue background, negative words in gold letters. A feeling of oppression made him look around in search of the others whom he knew were nearby. But he didn't see anybody, except for the same indistinct group. Half reluctantly he then imagined a rough sketch of the coprophilic scene, the rocking chair and the gears of the waterwheel. He found a somewhat hazy connection between the present dream and the coprophilic scene, even though he could determine nothing. He experienced a bunch of chaotic ideas which were lately bothering the normal rhythm of his days. He only knew that between the more or less spontaneous, more or less mechanical prayer and the action of the guy who had thrown himself upon his groin, there was a connection a little more important than the vague images which up until then had been conveyed to him. He pressed the nape of his neck upon the edge of the marble sill in search of a more violent pain that might suggest to him something between that and the rocking chair, between the rocking chair and the waterwheel. But the pain only made him tremble and threw him into the previous dream with the violence of one who rejects an excessive intervention. As he stirred in the deck chair, waking up already in the middle of the third dream, he kept deep inside the hurt of one who is rejected by something basic, concrete, elementary, but necessary, profoundly necessary. The canvas was rough and the sharp edges of the frame hurt and the pegs squeaked, creating disjointed motions at the slightest adjustment when seated. The more uncomfortable the situation the greater the need to alter it, commensurate with the pain. In returning to this dream he noticed a slight modification. To his right there was a window with the shutters closed. He now knew about the existence of this window, but he didn't see it. Not that it was nonexistent, it may have been replaced by another element, a wall, for example, but he simply didn't see it. He ensconced himself in the best manner possible on the stiff canvas of the deck chair and managed to establish an affinity between the coprophilic moment, the prayer, and the gears of the waterwheel. Only the rocking chair was left. And this leftover made him so agitated that he overturned the deck chair. Hurt, he lifted himself up in front of a window, but was already in the second dream. A large window, to be precise. A wide and tall panel of opaque green glass encased in thin strips of black iron. In the middle, similar to a window within the window, there was an asymmetrical arrangement of small pieces of white glass, also opaque, milky. From the waist up two rectangles juxtaposed by a black line. At foot level, to the left three vertical rectangles and to the right two squares. At the height of his ankles a milky strip extended from end to end. He was returning exactly to the same position and to the same preoccupations of the second dream. Of all the dreams it was the one that pleased him the most. So at that moment, it was with a certain relief that he saw himself once again in front of the large window. If on the trip going only a reality of lines, a landscape without shadows or oscillations, a landscape only of color, on the return trip, without even formulating anything coherently, merely juxtaposing reminiscences of the other dreams, he was living a more compact reality, loaded with the gears of the waterwheel, the rocking chair, the pressure of the lips on his penis, the hint of an arcade saturated with negative words, the collapse of the deck chair, a smoother reality that didn't go to the point of demanding explanations, but merely manifesting its presence. The only difference was a gradation in the intensity of how he was seeing things. And by now his gaze was more fierce. Without looking for a definition or for words, he was moved by a heap of emotions, as yet unknown. For that very reason he understood perfectly, already into the first dream, the violent act of his closed fist which did not get to shatter the glass, but did remain in the middle of the panel like fleshy sun and its fractured sunbeams. He was still rubbing his wrist and the joints of his fingers which, in the dream he was awakening from, had hit the large window. He stirred in the chair and only then did he observe with alarm that, upon falling asleep and taking part in the first dream, he hadn't even grasped its substance. Tall, with carved arms ending in swirls on the seat, the high chairback sculpted at the top, and arched feet tapering into paws of three claws. In front of him a two-year-old child was walking very hesitantly in the room while stretched out in the corner a cougar purred and rubbed its snout with its paw. A wave of humor engulfed him and he leaned on the chairback, assuming an attitude that fit his delirium, remembering the other reality and at this point a vocabulary that was really clear to him. Only his humor altered the sacred gestures he was rehearsing for an opportune moment. He felt the approach of a man from behind and began to hear some words at the exact moment the child stepped on the cougar's tail and the animal pawed the kid, knocking him down. The man behind kept insisting upon something urgent. He struggled to look for a link between an animal's pawing, the blow against the large window, the collapse of the deck chair, the prayer, the pressure of the lips, the rocking chair, and the waterwheel. The man persisted. He became irritated. He didn't want to hear him. He woke up. Stretched out in a hotel cubicle, a little bit wider than a bed, the ceiling seemed to him more remote than it actually was. There was no fatigue or torpor but clearheadedness. On the chair stuck between the bed and the opposite wall, he found the cigarette and the match. The pear-shaped light switch was above the entrance of the door and he didn't feel like moving. He smoked in what still seemed to be nighttime. But as he reached the middle of the cigarette a dim light gave better definition to the cubicle. He stood up. He got dressed and went out. The city was sleeping in the midst of ruins and hovels. A wild wind blew the dust, with difficulty his shoes moved forward upon the unpaved streets, sometimes full of holes, sometimes covered with a shiny gravel or with pieces of glass, or so it seemed to him. The shops would soon be opening their doors and the men who dreamed so much of long ago splendors would again assume their job of extracting from the subsoil some mineral or other, accursed like the one of bygone days. He remembered the features of the old man who had kept him company for dinner the night before. He annoyed the owner of the hotel who was still sleeping when he demanded his bill. He walked up to the roadway and began to smoke until the arrival of the bus that would take him back. On the way he entirely lost his desire to formulate some idea of his problem and didn't give any importance to his dreams. A passenger was insulting the busdriver. You should go a little faster, step out of that snail's pace. He smoked and suddenly a tremor gave him the sensation of an inverted reality. Maybe he was beginning the first dream of seven others, but descending dreams, negative, impregnated with his quotidian behavior.

FAITH IN ONE'S CRAFT

I have before me two character sketches and a half sketch of a setting, and I don't know why I must stick to some convention of the short story, which by the way has no rules, and introduce the story only after solving in detail the enigmas the characters and the settings represent. Maybe this way of thinking explains my desire to exert my will upon the figures of fiction, and along these lines, to take away from them the autonomy they naturally should have. Which I suppose is another convention. In my desire to disregard conventions, I only fear I may be falling into a trap, that is, writing within another convention, previous to the first ones. If that is true, I beg your indulgence, given that the page must never be left blank. But that may not actually be a convention.

As a constant, the two figures manifest some form of insanity. The first one doesn't know whether it's really a white horse of a famous general or a puddle of water; the second one permanently oscillates between two sexes, which probably will arouse some psychoanalyst's sense of greed. The setting is composed of some real parallel lines, as well as false ones, some convergent, yet others divergent, some more or less regular prisms arranged at certain points in a spontaneously chaotic manner, and at others in an organized chaotic manner, and some cylinders which cross at a certain height. I would like to populate it with specters but I'm afraid their presence would bother the two figures, and that each specter may want to exert some influence upon each one of the figures in such a way as to make it into its own image and likeness. There are no vestiges of animals, eliminated due to a series of reasons and rules. The only mementos are small statuettes arranged in some of the sections of the prisms, purposely designed for the distraction of hypothetical children. There are no children. From the start two paths occur to me: either I develop a story within certain schemes very dear to the masters of psychology, and obviously of pathology, a path fertile and rich in suppositions, schemes, imaginations, deductions, and oneiric associations, and even more rich in histrionic motivations, or instead I opt for the second one which is to try and understand the character from its own genesis, involving the author, a barren path, at times sterile and of diminished imaginative potential. I opt for the second one, up to the point it is possible to opt, up to the point where I myself cannot be transformed into fertile material for the followers of the first path. Given that some time ago I chose the path of indifference, I suppose, in truth, there really isn't an option, and in choosing the second path perhaps I am following a third. Under the pretense of consolation, what remains for me is the hope of some day finding a good essay on a treatise of superfluidity.

In cases like these the first thing to decide upon is the character's occupation. A character lives, eats, dresses, and though insane, needs money to cultivate its delusions. One of them, the one who doesn't know if it's the white horse of a famous general or a puddle of water, could be a drug dealer, one of white slaves, a smuggler of pearls or diamonds, an industrialist, the bill collector for a funeral agency, or even a famous general who could have a white horse; it's a bit difficult to relate occupation to the delusions of a puddle of water, although it seems possible, if one had enough courage to overcome the obstacle of ridicule. By having concentrated its insanity upon the oscillation of genders, the second figure gives me the idea of a prostitute or a professional pederast, occupations more or less fitted to specific excesses and to the specific abolishment of basic dignities.

Afterwards comes the problem of action, and it seems to me difficult, inasmuch as I prefer the more barren path, to get the action started (for much action is motion) in a pleasing manner. Even more difficult is coming up with the pleasing features. If I go the route of the white horse of the famous general, my impulse is to really identify him with the white horse and to develop him in all his equine splendor, kicking and neighing at will. Only an optical illusion would preclude appreciating the beautiful mane, the shining hooves, and the intrepid neigh. The first path insinuates itself and brings me to treat him better as the famous general of the white horse. Seen from this angle it would be so very easy to set up some really absorbing episodes and by doing so contribute to the tedium of some good souls in search of harmonies. As for the puddle of water, where's the courage. To imagine its condition of water and puddle, eager for reflections and reëntrant angles, for very complicated motions and subtle ramifications, capable of a highly organized and extremely structured language, to imagine that condition is to make ill use of the admissible aridity in fiction. The second character presents the same difficulty. The first path fertile, the second barren. The first suggesting hybridity of oneiric forms, and the erudition of old mythologies, the second limited to the basic grasp of things. The first providing material for some good laughs with all the associations to different shapes, a mixture of mermaid and bull, a nymph from the navel down and a faun from the navel up. The second one doesn't give itself very well to digressions on the navel.

With the problem of action supposedly resolved, I would like to introduce only one idea for each character; it seems to me enough, albeit useless. On this point I would make one concession to my vanity, for nothing pleases me more than the discovery of some idea within the piece I am writing. Although at first sight it may seem easy, I confess that nothing is more arduous for me than to discover an idea. So, as an out, I would leave each character with only half an idea, or even a third, which happens to me quite often. Maybe the problem of the character who becomes delirious with the horse and the puddle of water is one of immortality; in that case, between aspiring to an eternal model of the horse and that of a puddle of water, I'll go for the puddle of water, and for the eternity of the two, puddle and water. I'll give in to the total impulse of my paranoia, and to the memory of two moments: one, in a dubious hotel in the Lapa district, where I glimpsed a gleam in the eyes of a so-called degenerate, another, under the colonnade entrance of a mosque in Nazareth, on the way to the Sea of Galilee, where an old man in rags was bending over in prayer on a rug. Both believed in immortality.

The dénouement could occur with the horse's hoof mounted by an hermaphrodite inside the puddle of water.

Lately a taste for ambiguous things, for useless meanings, for the useless synthesis of certain contradictions, leads me to accept the narrative's title in spite of hurting some people's olfactory sensibilities by some unexpected synesthesia.

THE FIRST CUP OF COFFEE

One still couldn't see the sun, but the light was strong when she opened the bedroom door to the living room. She buttoned her dress and went down the steps toward the bathroom in the backyard, past the tile roof that covered the washbasin. Beyond the wall to her left, from the extended roof of the side veranda which covered the neighbor's house, singing from the birdcages could be heard. In front, the fenced property contained some trees she did not recognize and some mounds of dirt, garbage, pieces of glass, empty cans. (She recalled the strange taste of a fruit they had given her in Dakar, greenish-yellow, with an enormous pit filled with fibers that got stuck in her teeth.) The evening before, she had not been able to see much of the house since it was already dark when she arrived. Enough time to open the boxes, crates, suitcases, to help make the beds for the master and children's bedrooms, to spread the bedsheets wrinkled from a long trip, and to improvise a recipe for soup with what was possible to find in the kitchen.

And to go to sleep to reencounter the man who years before had left in search of better fortune. While climbing the steps again to the kichen, the sun brightened the whitewash of the side wall and the opening of the door cast a distorted rectangle of light into a promise of peace. She filled the kettle with water, set it down, filled the stove with coal, kneaded some pages from an old newspaper, and struck them into the opening at the base. While the flame swept over the grayish new iron plating, she looked more carefully at the floor and the wall covered with tiles, the salt and pepper stone sink, the shelves where the night before she had placed in a somewhat disorderly fashion the pots, frying pans, dishes, utensils, and a few cans of food. Here they said the month of June was actually the end of October, the beginning of winter, nevertheless, the heat reminded her of the June from before, end of spring, beginning of summer. The large feathered pillows will still be able to be used, they were used to them, but the huge blankets will have to be put away or cut up and made into small cushions or extra pillows. The braided straw fan was to her side and with a bit of effort on her part the coal began to crackle, forcing her to actually step away from a spurt of sparks. Afterwards the stove became evenly hot and she could then cover the flames with the kettle. A hissing sound was heard, smoke spilled out from the stove and somebody coughed in one of the rooms. At that same hour she used to open her brother-in-law's store, while he lay stifling the cough that was killing his lung. As she left her house, rarely did she look around the square, at the hill to the left, the road to the woods beyond the store, the high walls of the cemetery not far from the synagogue. A sheet of newspaper catches her eye and carves persistently in her mind words she will have to learn. An illustrated page wrapping the package of eggs on top of the pine table, a picture of a woman, envelops her with the strong hope of a day not yet even formulated in her head, but somehow connected to the image of a veranda of a manor house embedded in a grove of chestnut trees, on the way to the small stream. The woman dressed in black with lace collar and cuffs, in a rocking chair with a book in her hands, and her gaze startled by the intrusion of people coming down the road. A dog growled in a corner of the veranda. That one was the tin for coffee; she measured the spoonfuls into the cloth filter just as they had taught her so that she could fill the coffeepot almost to the brim. While she was wiping off the coffee grinds spilt by her shaky hand, a memory came to life of some vague sense of longing for a pure show of affection. Something with the consistency of a reverie. An impulse in between terror and obedience. Merely an unsettling rumble on a snowy winter's night, of winter and snow gone once and for all, winter and snow never loved, because she never loved landscapes, but nevertheless a habit. It was while looking at the kettle, as she waited for the whistle of the boiling water, that she experienced that sense of definitive loss. They must all be awake by now. Somebody had definitely opened the door to the veranda. A rumbling on a winter's night. Her sister who one day gathers her belongings and at dawn leaves in a carriage. Her brother who doesn't even take his belongings. A sudden shudder as a presentiment of something beautiful in a certain unknown part of the world. There were moments on the ship, at night, while her children were asleep, when the rocking of the hull and the whoosh of the sea made her more certain of an inevitable feeling of disquiet. A mixture of digression and digestion of basic notions emanating from a folkloric tradition. A certain order for things. The sea. The sky. The fish. Life. A halo of myth and hope during a moment of abandonment. The steam violently shakes the cover of the kettle and escapes thickly through the spout. How pleasant the aroma of the coffee that begins to fill the pot. She places the cups in an orderly fashion, sweetens them, and is going to leave them on the dining table. Some members of the family settle in their chairs, others take their cups to the door of the veranda. All the birdcages of the neighbor's house are aflutter. Suddenly a look of disgust appears on everybody's face and they all put their cups down on the table. Only then did she bring her cup to her lips and something disturbing shook her whole body. She couldn't even manage to smile indulgently at herself.

"I wasn't familiar with salt so white and so refined!"

JOHNY *GOLEM*

A weariness and a kind of nausea lead me to pen the story of Johny *Golem*. A weariness brought on by an accumulation of trivial matters, nausea brought on by the infinite number of possibilities in human stupidity. May my few friends forgive me, I do not write for readers, I write for a few friends, may they forgive my tone, but for some time now I've been trying out platitudes and reinventions of the wheel. Only this solitude of the apartment in Ahusa, in between the vegetation of Mount Carmel and that of the distant strip of the Mediterranean with its taut surface gleaming under a winter sun, and the yearning for some things truly ancient, incite me to continue the writing of a story which at another point in time would seem to me banal. A lack of talent prevents me from choosing the path of science fiction, a path that would allow for exploitations and expansions of the episode, with a plunge into the outer limits of horror and pure fantasy, not to mention the other level of anticipation, aspirations a bit more natural than the refined thoughts of a misunderstood passion. The strangest thing of all is the chaotic way I became cognizant of all the episodes, a way that makes me doubt certain details, and also the fact that the few individuals who explained things to me spoke in French, English, Spanish, Yiddish, languages of which I was only able to decipher a few words. There are some humorous details. Some of the informants, also wanting more explanations, sometimes accompanied me to the residence of others, and on those occasions I tried to grasp some meaning from sentences spoken in Bulgarian, Romanian, Arabic, languages of which I am totally ignorant, except for the vague hint from a sound, or from some illusive syllables. Naturally the mistakes were tremendous, but the moments of humor were plentiful, and what stayed with me was the vague idea that for understanding certain essential states of being, all that is linked to speech, excluding the word, is more than sufficient.

My intent was to avoid explanations, but I believe that some prior information on the *golem*, although not helping very much to understand this case, and at the moment understanding doesn't interest me, on the other hand, does help the composition of the story, which written in any other way would seem to me to be somewhat wanting. I went to all the bookstores in Haifa in search of some information and I found nothing. Merely one bookseller's amazement at my interest in such an old topic. I am only making use of data collected from the Jewish Encyclopedia, found in the Pevsner Library. The first interesting piece of information is that the word appears only once in the Bible, in Psalm 139, verse 16, with the meaning of *embryo*. But the juicy part of its history really occurs in the Middle Ages when some men believed it was possible to give life to a human figure made of clay or wood. That figure of clay was given the name of *golem*. Splendid material for a fictional tale of horror or other incursions into the field of harrowing possibilities. The medieval atmosphere, with its vulgar and truculent style, but also with its mystical euphorias (today we merely operate by axiom), is suitable for those adventures. The lack of ability, however, in truly composing a story for the delight of a few leads me always to go outside the path of authentic creation, which gives me some consolation because I am certain I will never be tempted to create my own *golem*, inasmuch as creator and creature sometimes get confused. Moreover, there are certain gloomy areas so obvious that they escape the notice of those who go about in search of bottomless regions. Salomon in Gabirol was accused of having created his own *golem*, but he managed to prove the mistake. Rabbi Elijah of Chelm, Rabbi Elijah of Wilna, Rabbi Israel Baal-Shem Tov are considered the creators of identical figures, and the most known is Judah Löw of Prague. The last *golem* is attributed to Rabbi David Jaffe, of Grodno, Russia, around 1800. It was made by inserting into the mannequin's mouth or placing on its forehead a piece of paper which had a combination of letters forming a *shem* (one of God's infinite names). Let it be known as well that in today's vernacular, *golem* also means idiot.

I heard the first reference to Johny *Golem* in the Rondo, a restaurant-bar next to the Dan Carmel Hotel, on a Friday a little before eleven at night. I confess I am not sure if I really understood, but the whole case in itself is so confusing that I actually believe any change in detail due to ignorance is forgivable and insignificant. Paul Segall, a forty-two-year-old Englishman, short, slim, with thinning blondish-red hair, already half drunk, pronounced the word before beginning a conversation with me. He was in Haifa as a representative of an English company that wanted to set up a factory close to the Dead Sea, not exactly a factory of potash for one already existed there, but of certain derivatives which were combined with derivatives of petroleum. His job was to study the installation project and the possibility of utilizing a branch of the Eilat-Haifa pipeline oil system. At midnight we left the Rondo, and Segall suggested an Arabic bar where we could continue to drink. In the taxi, while we were leaving French

Carmel and were passing by the Baha'i Temple, Segall said the word *golem* two or three times. Leaning back against the car's upholstery he seemed to have reached the phase of inebriation that immediately precedes sleep. But near the bar he woke up completely. He ordered beer and shish-kabob and his light face brightened up again. When I saw he was in an almost normal state, I asked him what *golem* meant to him. Segall appears to become frightened but rapidly he regains his composure, and not holding back, he explodes into laughter. The summary of what I heard after is more or less the following, complete with the obligatory apologies for any mistake made in translation. Prior to working for the chemical factory, Segall used to belong to the Secret Service of His Majesty's Army. Homosexual, he found himself embroiled in a serious affair and was removed from his position. If his situation allowed him access to certain places, it also made him victim in that game of cat and mouse. The story about the *golem* was linked to his tenure in the Army and was one of the greatest failures of the research sector. Segall looked at his watch and in a semi-provocative manner decided to resort to the technique of Oriental storytellers. The rest of the story, it wasn't exactly a secret, could be told tomorrow on a bench in the small garden next to the Hotel Panorama. At ten-thirty sharp Segall appeared. It was a beautiful winter Saturday, cold and sunny. And he told me the rest of the story:

"I am humiliated as a human being, and not as a Jew, a Moham-medan, a Negro, a homosexual or a paralytic," this was the statement made by someone at the time, when the *golem* experiment was being developed. This statement became engraved in my mind, and per-haps because of it a residue of the actual word has stayed with me, which in other circumstances would be placed on the roster of things of vague interest to me. Segall spoke without looking at me, his at-tention caught by the movement of a branch that was tilting gently under the weight of a bird.

Brice Account was a mediocre, meticulous man, the type known for rigorously fulfilling his obligation. In my opinion he always went around hoping for an opportunity to gain fame. His break came by way of an army hospital patient. Brice headed one of the research sectors of the Secret Service, linked to the possible uses of psychology in case of war, for individual as much as group situations. The patient, a Jew from the poor district, was part of a group that had come from Poland a few years ago. Till today I still do not know how he ended up in the army hospital, perhaps due to the protection of some official, or something like that. He was a schizophrenic, with strong bouts of paranoia, besides being epileptic. I think that's the way they classified him. I don't remember his name, if at one point I ever really got to know it. After a given period, the name we all knew him by was Johny *Golem*. During the few times Brice had a conversation with the patient, contradictory feelings would take place within him. The chaotic speech, alternating silences and chaotic loquacity. A pornographic explosion of words counterbalanced with mystical ecstasies, providing a picture impossible to look at without laughing. The man's English was terrible and anything he would say was incomprehensible. Brice asked the advice of a Jewish friend and this guy vouched that even the Yiddish spoken by Johny *Golem* was garbled. But on the advice of this same Jewish friend, a psychiatrist with a good middle-class practice, Brice became interested in certain aspects of Jewish life in Poland, Russia, etc. He asked for my help in his research and I believe I was the one who furnished him with the data on Rabbi Löw. It was then that Brice burned the midnight oil over his spectacular plan. (Segall smiled slightly and regained his austere demeanor for the statement that follows.) I don't want to judge Brice, there are certain problems linked to state interests that are above the individual, therefore I do not want to classify my former boss's behavior as cruel. It would be infantile on my part to do so. Brice Account tried to transform the patient into an authentic *golem*, utilizing for that goal all the resources of his research sector. I attended one of those experiments and I believe that during one of them Johny, or somebody else, yelled out the inflated sentence I quoted above. There is still one other detail. Bob Smile was one of my colleagues at work, efficient, intelligent even though he wasn't very studious. Bob Smile provided Brice with another bit of information. He called his attention to the tremendous possibilities in expanding the concept of conditioned reflexes.

Segall went on and on about a series of professional details which, this neither being the time nor the place, will not be mentioned, except for an explanation about certain relations between behavior and depth of the mind, a tiresome explanation like all purely professional accounts. The story continued properly when he told me that Johny had been released from the hospital and he went back to live among his own. Use was made of secret agents and all the tools readily available today to any middle-school student—tape recorders, portable and minuscule transmitters, and above all, a machine for producing noises and sounds with high and low vibrations capable of being caught by the human ear. Johny walked around the city as a real village idiot. Sometimes Brice was thrilled with the results, other times he grew desperate with what seemed to him, in relation to his scientific experiment, an excessive degree of freedom on the part of the *Golem*. Segall remembered there were some grotesque episodes, even though he could not summarize them. He only knew that some of the people who were acquainted with Johny and Brice now lived in Haifa, and he didn't know whether to classify that turn of events as ironic or coincidental. At that very moment he offered to accompany me to the house of one of those people.

The taxi left us near the entrance of a nursing home for the elderly, and a few moments later we were in a large living room in the company of a short, thin man, slightly bald and with a small whitish beard. He was Werner Huhn. Afterwards Segall explained to me that Huhn had been a disciple of Jung and, being weary and discontent, he withdrew into the life of an old man who is merely waiting for death to come. Segall and Huhn conversed for a long time in German, they laughed a lot. Segall forgot to translate their conversation for me. He only said that Huhn had been consulted by Brice apropos certain details, and by all indication Brice didn't understand any of the explanation.

The next visit was to a big old house near the port. A fat and jolly woman received Segall with fanfare, more out of habit than intimacy. They spoke in Hungarian. At a certain moment the two of them burst into raucous laughter, the old woman slapping her thighs and shaking her sagging and enormous breasts, Segall bending over and squirming. As we left he explained to me that Johny *Golem* at one time decided to fall in love with a nonexistent daughter of Brice. The old woman, who used to clean house for Johny's relatives, witnessed the whole passionate affair. (Segall let it be known that she had also taken part in Brice's plan, in exchange for a few English pounds.)

After the old woman we went to meet a male nurse at the Bat-Galim hospital. He had worked in the army hospital and remembered the episode when Johny *Golem* tried to kill Brice with a two-by-four. Brice scurried about terrified, wagging his rump in search of cover.

While we were having coffee back again in Carmel, Segall ended the story: Brice went berserk, but not like a spell that turns against the sorcerer; after all, Johny was incapable of doing anything. What really happened is that Bob Smile took over his post and Segall presumes that Bob must have applied to Brice the methods he had applied to Johny.

I end the story at this point, by now totally disinterested. I still refrain from relating a few episodes, episodes which occurred after I lost sight of Segall, like what happened in a café in Naples while absentmindedly I scribbled Johny *Golem's* name on a napkin and the waiter laughed and agreed to a rendezvous with me that same night; the episode with Nenna, a forty-year-old woman who worked in the laundry of the Stazione Termini in Rome, and who with a suggestion from the Neapolitan waiter gave me some more details; the episode with Schlomo, the broadcasting technician with whom I spoke on Caumartin Street in Paris; and the episode with Gama Silveira, the Brazilian who knew Bob Smile, and who now works for a firm located beyond the Chiado Plaza in Lisbon. Nausea, fatigue, and this cigarette smoke rising serenely on the veranda tell me that it's time to stop. Time to dot a period.

LISBON BY NIGHT

He found only one empty place at the bar. Between a tall, blond, robust fellow and an old whore. Both were having beer. He sat down and also ordered a beer. He drank half a glass and turned around supporting his back against the edge of the counter. The main dance floor was full as were the surrounding tables. Between the blare of the orchestra playing a mambo, he heard shouts in English, French, and German. The women were almost all Portuguese. There was only one Spanish woman and one Italian. Though clinging to a sailor in the corner of the dance floor, one of them waved to him just the same, amidst the laughter, her left hand in a fist, swaying back and forth like a doll's head. He responded by puffing up his cheeks and vehemently blowing out the air, a gesture that always brought on a burst of laughter from the woman.

"Aren't you going to offer me a beer, Isaac."

The old whore gave him a poke with her elbow.

"You know me?"

"You have been coming here everyday for the past four months, I lie, you didn't show up twice."

"Good observer!"

"I have plenty of time on my hands!"

A band of tall blond men in street clothes entered the bar, bursting with laughter.

"By the looks of things, this is going to be jam-packed with Swedes." After emptying her glass, the old whore remained in the same position as he did, leaning against the bar, facing the entrance, her legs crossed.

"Some ship in port?"

"It docked this afternoon."

"Funny, I don't remember you."

"My tough luck, my Brazilian."

The youngest guy in the band of Swedes approached her and placed both of his hands on her thighs. She wrapped her arms around his neck and bit him lightly on the ear.

"Long live Portiugaaal!" yelled the Swede, hugging and lifting her quite high before putting her down. *"Let's go dance!"*

Still laughing, he twisted around and filled his glass again. Of all the bars on Sodré Wharf this is the one he preferred. It had fewer mirrors, more lights, and it was the widest, a detail that let him observe the whole room from the bar. Only now had he realized what she said. In four months, he had only missed two nights. Besides this cozy corner what pleased him most was the *Solar da Madragoa*, with the really short and buxom Hilde Silva, all riled up, tackling a fado song with the vigor and rage of a grouchy woman from the Minho or the Alentejo provinces, or who knows where. His initial plans vanished during the first weeks. To research material for a novella on the Inquisition and to see the rest of the country, Évora, Nazaré, Braga. He was surrendering to the city in the same way he gave into the other places. Only in a more lackadaisical manner. Wake up at noon. Have coffee at the *Suiça* café in Rossio Square, go up the Avenida da Liberdade, spend the afternoon reading in the Eduardo VII Park, reading or brooding over old hatreds, having dinner at seven, then returning to the boardinghouse for a nap before going out again around ten o'clock. A movie. The bars. Fado houses.

"You're Brazilian, and your name is Isaac?" The accent was heavy on the R's, albeit not very strong. "Did you come to Lisbon for pleasure?"

"No! To hang out!"

The tall, blond, robust fellow to his left guffawed loudly and kept repeating, "to hang out, to hang out," until he asked:

"What does 'to hang out' really mean?"

He laughed even more when he got the sexual explanation, slapped him several times on the back and introduced himself as Johansen, a Dutch resident of Portugal for almost fifteen years.

"I never heard that expression around here!"

"I learned it in Rio, I don't know if it's used in Portugal, I'll ask about it one of these days."

The Swede came back with the whore, ordered two drinks and wished everybody a *Happy New Year* and *Merry Christmas*, spilled a bit of whiskey into Isaac's and Johansen's glasses of beer, shouting euphorically, *it's good, it's good, Portiugaaal,* and again dragged the woman to the dance floor.

A brief silence and smiles while they drank the mixed drinks.

"You are Brazilian and your name is Isaac?"

"Jewish!"

"Jewish?"

"Brazilian."

"Brazilian?"

Silence. Pause. Johansen orders a fresh glass and another beer, two in fact, he offers one to Isaac. A mambo is being played with the musicians singing backup. Suddenly, a woman's scream and a slap across the face of the scrawny kid who had whacked her. He was drunk. The Angolan negro came from his post at the door and without crumpling his uniform picked him up by the collar and the seat of his pants, crossed the room with him, and what one heard afterwards was only the impact of a body hitting the sidewalk. The orchestra continued to play the mambo. Isaac and Johansen drank.

"Jewish?"

"Jewish!"

"Brazilian?"

He took a pack of cigarettes out of the pocket of his jacket, offered one to Johansen who lit both of them. He unzipped his jacket, he was beginning to feel warm, but on the street, even though it was May, he still felt cold in the early morning air. The time when he used to ask an infinite number of questions about the numerous possibilities of who might be by his side, had passed. Now it was Johansen, he said he was Dutch, settled in Lisbon almost fifteen years ago, the month was May, the place, Sodré Wharf, and they were smoking and drinking together. In Brazil, when he walked up Mauá Square, he used to think only about the Inquisition, to see the places, to gather information, to search for books, to take note of the details on torture and the processions at the executions. A week later, facing a glass of brandy, in the middle of winter, he realized he didn't have a vocation for research, that the Inquisition was a remote subject, and to a certain extent infantile, that there were other things to see. In between laziness and intensity, a crazy whim to see the promontory at Sagres, but merely a whim. He even dreamed about Prince Henry the Navigator, with that same hat or whatever appeared in the engravings, a piece of cloth falling over to the left, to the right? But he didn't go south to the Algarve. He scribbled something down then tore it up. The updated version of a Czech legend. To write a history of the Brazilian Northeast bandits and the fertile land, the massapê, that's what he could not do. He never left Rio before this trip. He didn't even know São

Paulo. To write was merely an aspiration, a very nebulous desire he thought about each night as he left the advertising firm that had employed him. He still had two months ahead of him and was worried about the dwindling cash he had managed to save for his six-month leave. He thought he would be in his element writing a story about the Inquisition, he could fuse personal episodes, family figures, his parents were Romanians, stories told to him about persecutions, *autos-da-fé*. He was thirty years old, had some ambition, but he didn't have a very good idea of what it meant to be a writer. At the beginning of the trip he thought there was time, plenty of time, something he never had. Now he had too much and look what happened. Nothing! At least he learned one thing during those four months, maybe writing was nothing like what he expected it to be, and what he had seen all around him, and perhaps this really was the best part, was this nothingness, this emptiness. If the rest of the stuff had to come, it would come spontaneously.

"Jewish?"

"Jewish!"

"Brazilian?"

He began to find Johansen amusing. The tall swagger, stout, the high blond wave in his hair, and the good posture. Holland was a good country. Tulips. But he wouldn't go to Holland. He was much too lazy. It was enough to be sitting there chatting with a Dutchman. Holland was really what they said it was, dikes, canals. Spinoza, he now remembered. With a slip of fate that poor guy could have been Portuguese. But instead, he went to Holland to be born. Did you know about Spinoza? Yes, Johansen knew many things. Isaac remained silent, drinking his beer, the orchestra changing from mambos to blues, blues to waltzes, waltzes to sentimental Italian songs, he remained silent, drinking beer, smoking, while Johansen spoke! Spinoza, Kant, Bach, Sartre's latest book, Bergman's latest film which hadn't been shown in Lisbon, but he knew about it from a French magazine. Johansen talked, he was well traveled, he knew all of Europe, he spent vacations in England, France, and Italy. No, he didn't want to go back to Holland. His family *kaput* in the War. Johansen talked, talked, talked, Isaac remained silent, drinking beer, the orchestra playing, drinking beer and smoking, Johansen talking.

"Jewish?"

"Jewish!"

"Brazilian?"

Suddenly he seemed to see a wince of fear in Johansen. New silence. He was no longer talking. He was smoking. He was drinking. He was looking at him with an air of intrigue that was well disguised.

"I'm going off, I'm going to eat something!"

They paid the bill, Isaac still saw the Swede clinging to the old whore, dancing and shouting *Happy New Year, Portiugaaal.* They went to eat shrimp and codfish balls at an establishment next door. They drank white wine. Johansen began to interrogate him. What did he do? Where was he from? He didn't find it inconvenient to reply. Brazilian, advertising man, he was on vacation and had come to Lisbon to hang out.

"Jewish?"

"Jewish!"

"Brazilian?"

Johansen tried to say goodbye, he wanted to go home. Isaac insisted. Why couldn't they go on drinking? They went to one bar in the Alfama district, darker, smaller, they sat down at a table with two women and then Johansen changed completely. He hugged the two women, kissed them, began to tell dirty jokes, he drank seven or eight shots of whiskey, and sang a beautiful German song, after shouting a request for the orchestra to accompany him. A good baritone. Applause from everywhere. Johansen toppled on to the table, he seemed to be dozing. The women went on to another table, they had forgotten to order drinks for them. Isaac had drunk very little. He was clearheaded. He saw Johansen bent over the table, his hands fallen by his side, the wave in his hair messed up. But he was wrong, he wasn't dozing. In a flash he lifted his head, an aged face, eyes open, his voice hoarse.

"You don't know what hate is, Isaac, or fear! Who are you?"

"Brazilian!"

"Jewish?"

"Jewish!"

"Brazilian?"

"Brazilian!"

"Do you have a passport?"

He showed him his passport while he ordered a whiskey. He had been shaken by all this. The questionable doubts came up again. Who was Johansen? *What* was Johansen? He got his passport back, stuck it in the inside pocket of his jacket, and continued to stare at a face he did not know, aged, scared, tired.

Johansen wiggled, grabbed Isaac's glass, and emptied it in one gulp. Now he was determined to leave. The singer in the band came over to ask him if he wanted to sing something else. Johansen smiled, thanked him, straightened himself with a forceful yawn, arranged his hair with his fingers, and Isaac saw him as before, the younger face, without fatigue, like at Sodré Wharf, only with a tenseness in his face he already recognized, and a clearheaded look easily wiped off with merely a half a glass of booze. They left. In the taxi he sensed Johansen's nervousness but he agreed to go on drinking. They took a street that crossed the Avenida da Liberdade. An enormous cabaret, too much lighting, noisy, they arrived in the middle of the show. A very short singer, skeletal, with a carnation in his lapel, romantically warbled a song by Aznavour. They ordered beer. Johansen began to talk again. He spoke as before, excessively, overexcited, his face even more youthful, he only spoke about Jews, he really praised them, he bent over backwards with compliments, only Isaac caught sight of the clichés. But he wasn't the Johansen from before, he didn't show the spontaneity of the Johansen at Sodré Wharf. He was a man who was now getting worked up, one step from losing control.

"Are you Jewish, Johansen?"

"No, but I would like to be."

After the singer, came the songstress, then an illusionist, then a contortionist, then a comedian, then the singer again with another song by Aznavour. *Isaac, you don't know what hate or fear is!* Johansen got up and went to the bathroom. Isaac paid the bill and remained seated. When he saw Johansen leave the bathroom and go in the direction of the exit without looking at him, he got up and followed him. Together they went down a steep street and arrived at the Avenida. It was cold. Three, four o'clock in the morning? He pulled his zipper up to his collar. Johansen was in shirt sleeves and seemed to feel nothing. He was trying to hide an uneasiness. He hailed a taxi and without saying a thing sat in the backseat, trying to stop Isaac from getting inside. With a little bit of force, he grabbed onto the door and managed to get into the taxi.

"What are you afraid of, Johansen?"

"*You all* pursue me!"

"*You all* who, Johansen?"

Isaac asked the taxi driver to take them to the Portas de Santo Antão Street. The small bar and restaurant should still be open. Johansen leaned his arms on the back of the front seat with his head in his arms, he seemed to be sobbing. They got out of the cab and sat down at the first table in the only row next to the bar stools. When he ordered shrimp and a bottle of white wine, Isaac had already dismissed the possibility of paranoia.

"*You all* who, Johansen?"

In a few minutes Johansen emptied the bottle. He ordered a cognac. Two. Another bottle of wine. A whiskey.

"You are Brazilian and your name is Isaac?"

"Jewish!"

"Jewish?"

"Brazilian!"

"Brazilian? And the others?"

"What others?"

"Are they close by?"

"There are no others, Johansen, I am alone."

"I hate you, Isaac, I hate the Jews! They're after me!"

"Are you Dutch, Johansen?"

"No! I am German!"

He leaned his shoulders against the side wall and stretched his legs. He was completely drunk, completely, his head swayed, his hands trembled. Only his voice remained unchanged, a metallic speech.

"Johansen, I know what fear and hate are!"

Johansen was talking to himself in a low voice. There was nobody at the bar. The waiter had slipped to the back and the man at the register seemed to be out of it.

"Hatred remains but fear is exhausting, it pulverizes, and in a moment of weakness we even destroy ourselves and surrender."

A laugh took hold of his entire body, a laugh infectious to Isaac, and in the middle of their loud laughter, Johansen had stretched his two arms on to Isaac's shoulders, and while staring at each other, laughing, amid guffaws, Johansen shouted:

"I am a Nazi, I hate all of *you people*, and *you people* have finally located me."

The man at the register got scared, the waiter came out from the back.

"It's nothing, don't worry, he's half drunk. The bill!"

They passed Rossio Square and made their way in the direction of the Chiado. Johansen placed his right hand on his shoulder and followed along swaying to and fro. Isaac forcibly repressed a spate of ideas, both vague and clear, confused feelings, and very distinct passions, a whole torrent of emotions revolving around one name alone.

"Where are *they?*"

He lit several cigarettes while they walked in silence, aimlessly crossing streets, going backwards, stumbling into alleys. In his innocence, or supposed innocence, he reinvented various childhoods and fused everything into a world which produced that guy by his side, into a world which permitted everything and, instead of waking up from the nightmare, merely exchanged nightmares. Still walking aimlessly, they went back to Rossio Square. Isaac hailed a taxi and settled Johansen in the back, telling the driver to take him home, he would give him the address. Joahnsen was sobbing in the back seat, sobbing loudly.

"You're not going to take me away, you're not going to arrest me? Why?"

He slammed the door violently, the cab pulled away in a rush.

He took the street in the direction of the square next to the river and stopped near the ferry dock for Cacilhas. Dawn was coming up. The surrounding hills appeared. A group of laborers embarked on the first launch that had arrived. When he made his way back to the boardinghouse he wasn't very sure if there were any seagulls, but of one thing he was certain. He would never write the novel on the Inquisition.